THE KILLER NEXT DOOR

Leaning against the wall next to the third door, Clint held his breath and listened carefully for a moment. He could definitely hear someone moving inside that room.

When the gunshots came, the sound of them exploded through Clint's head in much the same way the bullets exploded through the thin wooden wall. He recoiled from where he'd been standing.

He would have returned fire, but he couldn't see a target. All he could see were the holes being punched through the wall, working their way closer to where he was standing.

DON'T MISS THESE ALL-ACTION WESTERN SERIES FROM THE BERKLEY PUBLISHING GROUP

THE GUNSMITH by J. R. Roberts

Clint Adams was a legend among lawmen, outlaws, and ladies. They called him . . . the Gunsmith.

LONGARM by Tabor Evans

The popular long-running series about Deputy U.S. Marshal Long—his life, his loves, his fight for justice.

SLOCUM by Jake Logan

Today's longest-running action Western. John Slocum rides a deadly trail of hot blood and cold steel.

BUSHWHACKERS by B. J. Lanagan

An action-packed series by the creators of Longarm! The rousing adventures of the most brutal gang of cutthroats ever assembled—Quantrill's Raiders.

DIAMONDBACK by Guy Brewer

Dex Yancey is Diamondback, a Southern gentleman turned con man when his brother cheats him out of the family fortune. Ladies love him. Gamblers hate him. But nobody pulls one over on Dex. . . .

WILDGUN by Jack Hanson

The blazing adventures of mountain man Will Barlow—from the creators of Longarm!

TEXAS TRACKER by Tom Calhoun

Meet J. T. Law: the most relentless—and dangerous—manhunter in all Texas. Where sheriffs and posses fail, he's the best man to bring in the most vicious outlaws—for a price.

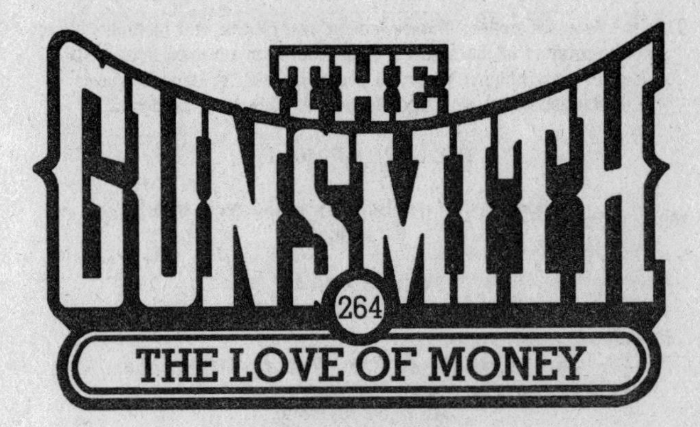

J. R. ROBERTS

JOVE BOOKS, NEW YORK

THE LOVE OF MONEY

A Jove Book / published by arrangement with
the author

PRINTING HISTORY
Jove edition / December 2003

For information address: The Berkley Publishing Group,
a division of Penguin Group (USA) Inc.,
375 Hudson Street, New York, New York 10014.

ISBN: 0-515-13642-5

A JOVE BOOK®
Jove Books are published by The Berkley Publishing Group,
a division of Penguin Group (USA) Inc.,
375 Hudson Street, New York, New York 10014.
JOVE and the "J" design
are trademarks belonging to Penguin Group (USA) Inc.

PRINTED IN THE UNITED STATES OF AMERICA

10 9 8 7 6 5 4 3 2 1

ONE

Clint had been riding south for a couple of days. Taking his time and enjoying the ride, he worked his way into northern California as the winter lost more and more of its bite. The days were getting easier to bear and the wind was becoming cool instead of bone-chillingly cold. He welcomed the difference, just as he welcomed the beautiful sight of the Sierras, which hung in front of him like a huge, snowcapped promise in the distance.

In that part of the country, he didn't have to wait long before reaching the next town. In fact, there were so many settlements scattered thereabouts that the only time he camped at all was when he felt like spending a night under the stars rather than on a rented mattress.

But the towns weren't exactly the biggest or most luxurious. Most of them were boom towns that had sprung up on the hopes and dreams of a few like-minded settlers who'd struggled across the country in search of better things. Oftentimes, they found something that wasn't quite what they were after, but was good enough to build a house around and stake a claim. Some folks settled for mines of various types, ranging from silver to coal, with several valuables in between. Some towns were simply built around a river that was strong enough to power a mill, and some had been born on more prominent finds.

The ultimate prize, of course, had been gold. That was what had caused most travelers to drag themselves and their families over rugged terrain and through unfriendly locals. Gold was the thing most settlers had in common. Even if some of the men and women in those wagon trains from years ago had said they were after a better life, they were thinking about something much more solid.

Solid gold.

Riding through the scenic country, Clint could see why so many had been drawn to California and were still coming in waves of weary, anxious faces. The land was rich and fertile, looking like a pretty face on a beautiful woman. Even if it lived up to only half its potential, surely the rewards would be worth the risk.

At least, that's what those people thought. Dreams like that had a way of withering on the vine. The sad fact was that reality had a nasty habit of showing its true face in a powerful fashion. Even worse was that by the time those realities sunk in, it was usually too late to turn back.

Whole families were buried on the trail leading to gold country. Those families that did survive were usually less a few members and would never be the same again. But they were tougher and their dreams were even more powerful after having made it through such a test. After all, once someone endured so much and got to set their sights on land as beautiful and rich as California, who could blame them for thinking the worst was behind them?

Even as he thought about those things, Clint tossed around the idea of going after some of the gold that was surely still buried in the dirt, at the bottom of streams or in the mountains themselves. He smiled and shook his head, feeling like a kid who'd sat down to his first faro game with a few hard-earned dollars in his hand.

He'd heard about those that had lost, but the stories of

those that had won easily outshone them. If he closed his eyes, he could just about feel his winnings in his pocket. He could already smell the money, and the only true guarantee he had was that he would definitely not get any of it unless he tried.

But Clint was no wide-eyed kid being suckered in by fast-talking dealers or even the sight of money just out of his reach. He'd sat in on plenty of games and knew that in faro, just like the chase for gold, all of the odds favored the house.

When someone stuck their tin pan into the river or started chipping away at a mountainside, the house they were playing against was the land itself. And no matter how beautiful it was, it was more merciless than any dealer.

Some beautiful women might have wicked minds, just like some dealers might be palming cards or stacking the deck. Mother Nature was all of those things, plus she had the advantage of not having a conscience. That was a dangerous combination, which made Clint set aside the thought of trying his luck against her and decide to simply enjoy his ride.

In that part of the country, though, there were plenty of folks who thought about it differently. The results they got could even be seen in the names of the towns that Clint had passed through over the last week or two.

There were towns like Broken Back, Busted Wheel, and Dead Horse, which were every bit as dreary and run-down as their names suggested. For every one of those, on the other hand, there were towns like Miller's Strike, Silverton, and Paradise Found, which told a much cheerier tale of founders who'd gotten a better life at the end of their journey.

In the end, all that mattered was that those folks had loaded up their wagons and set out in search of something.

Whether they found it or not was never as important as the fact that they gave it their best shot.

Busted Wheel was actually a bigger town than Miller's Strike. And Paradise Found had some of the shabbiest hotel beds Clint had ever tried to rest his back on. Clint visited each of them in turn, making his way through the beautiful country just like so many others who'd come before him. Although he wasn't in search of gold or silver, he still felt the pull of the riches in Mother Nature's pockets.

After all, when looking around at the splendor of the thick forests and awe-inspiring mountains, who wouldn't think they'd found some sort of promised land? Knowing as much as he did after listening to plenty of those travelers' stories, Clint still didn't blame them for trying their luck and slapping their chips onto the table.

Things didn't always turn out for the worse. Sometimes even the longest odds paid out, and when they did, the victory seemed all the more glorious.

Clint could see a town not too far ahead. He'd been steering Eclipse toward it all morning. Now that he was close enough to see the people walking from place to place, he spotted a sign on the side of the road. It read, "Welcome to Richwater."

Taking the name of the place as a good omen, Clint snapped his reins and rode onto the rutted street.

TWO

"You're damn lucky you got that preacher there beside you, or you'd be dead where you stand."

The man who'd spat that threat out from between thin lips was of average height and had a build that would have been muscular only by a scarecrow's standards. His clothes were threadbare and hanging off his body, and he wore a hat to cover his balding head from the wind. That same wind came by to knock the hat off his head, exposing the ring of dark hair around the bald top.

Standing on the row of planks that made up the walkway that stretched along Main Street, the balding man took a quick look over his shoulder to see where his hat had gone. Burning with anger, he turned his eyes back to another, shorter man who stood no more than seven to ten feet in front of him.

"Take it easy, Eddie," the shorter man said. "Nobody has to lose their temper here."

"Too late for that," Eddie replied. "Now hand over what you owe me before someone gets hurt. And when I say someone, I mean you."

Both of those men stood in front of a large building marked by painted letters as the Richwater Dry Goods

Store. The store was the biggest on a street made up mostly of little places specializing in clothing repair or more specialized needs. Across the way was a row of businesses ranging from a lawyer to an undertaker.

The street itself was just wide enough for a wagon and a horse to pass each other, bordered by thick wooden planks that were only kept in place by the constant pummeling of pedestrian feet. In the couple of seconds that had passed since Eddie first raised his voice, people had poked their noses out of nearly every store to watch the scene. Some locals even stood outside to get a better view.

Apart from Eddie and the man he was yelling at, there was one more man standing at the center of attention. That man was a bit taller than Eddie and had thick, light brown hair. The simple black clothes he wore made him appear even leaner than he was, and the white collar made him hold his chin up high. He'd been standing with both hands held at his sides, but raised them in a soothing gesture when tempers started to flare.

It was this preacher who stepped forward just as Eddie gritted his teeth and started to grumble an angry curse.

"Come now, come now," the third man said as he put himself between the other two. "Let's not make hasty decisions before we take some time to think them through."

"I took all the time I needed, Preacher," Eddie said. "And while I was thinking, this here bastard has been doing everything but stealing the wood from my own fire."

"Surely that can't be so." Turning to the shorter man, the figure who'd appointed himself as mediator asked, "Is it, Will?"

Will's first impulse had been to back up a step once he saw Eddie coming toward him. Now that the preacher was in front of him, he held his ground and put on the same face he used when sitting in the uncomfortable pew every Sunday. "Of course it ain't true."

His lip curling a bit more, Eddie's entire body tensed as if he was about to throw himself at the other man no matter who'd put themselves in front of him.

Will saw that when he looked around the preacher's shoulders, and he quickly added, "Well, it's all not true. There might have been a misunderstanding is all."

"You hear that?" the preacher asked in a soothing voice. "A misunderstanding. Those happen to everyone from time to time."

"Well, they've been happening more and more whenever that little asshole is involved." Eddie sneered. His eyes darting over to the man in black, he mumbled, "Pardon my language."

The preacher nodded once and smiled comfortingly. "You are of course forgiven. Now, why can't we resolve this matter so easily?"

Although Eddie's face had lightened up a bit, he was a long way from forgiving anyone. That much was obvious by the way his nostrils flared and the veins stood out on his bare scalp. Suddenly, he eased himself back a step and nodded to the man in the black clothes and white collar.

"All right, Preacher," Eddie said in a voice that had become suddenly calm. "Step aside so I can forgive Will for what he done."

The preacher narrowed his eyes and started to lower his hands. "You promise to forgive him?"

"Yes, sir."

"And then this matter will be done?"

"It'll all be over."

Glancing over his shoulder, the preacher took one look at Will and let his hands drop. "All right, then." With that, he turned and stepped out from between the two men.

As soon as the preacher was clear, Eddie pulled the gun from his holster and took a quick shot at Will. The shot blasted through the air and a chunk of hot lead whipped from one man toward another. Smoke belched from the barrel of Eddie's gun, drifting up into the smile that had spread across his face.

Will staggered back, his heels scraping over the dirty boards wedged into the ground. One of his heels caught on the edge of a board and he fell back, while reaching with both hands to try and break his fall. When he landed, his hip hit the ground first and the rest of him wound up in an awkward bundle.

The preacher's face was pulled taut into a pale, shocked expression. Both hands had come up once again, as though he expected to catch the bullet before it could reach its intended target. But even as his hands reached forward, his feet carried him back. It seemed that no matter how good his intentions were, even he knew when it was too late.

For a moment, Will just lay on the ground. Then, after letting out a groaning breath, he rolled onto his belly.

"There," Eddie said smugly. "Now it's over."

THREE

Clint was just riding into town when he heard the shots. The sound of them seemed to rattle the rest of the place around him and was more than enough to shatter the peaceful mood he'd been in during his ride. When he looked around to see if he could find out where they'd come from, Clint saw nothing but a relatively empty street and a few locals who were just as confused as he was.

It didn't take long for the commotion to spread as one kid who looked to be about eight or nine years old came sprinting around the corner. The boy waved his arms wildly and began talking excitedly to the first familiar face he could find.

Although Clint couldn't hear what the kid was saying, he could see easily enough where he was pointing. Looking in that direction, he noticed a few other people headed that way, so he steered Eclipse there as well and snapped the reins. The Darley Arabian stallion responded as though he'd been ready for the command before Clint gave it. That was no surprise, since the horse was always ready for a good run.

Clint managed to keep the stallion from going full out, but he did allow him to put a bit of steam into his strides.

They covered the distance in no time at all, and Clint immediately picked out the source of the commotion when they came around the corner.

Despite the fact that Clint didn't recognize any of the faces or know what was going on, he could tell quite a lot from what he could see. There was one man lying on the ground, crumpled up as though he was wounded. Another taller man was walking toward him, pointing his gun down to the wounded man as if he meant to finish what he'd started.

What caught Clint's attention the most was the third man in the middle of the ruckus, who was dressed in the black clothing and white collar of a priest. Clint was still heading toward the three when he saw the priest jump in front of the man with the gun, holding his arms out as though he thought he could catch the next bullet that was fired.

If the taller man saw the priest, he gave no indication. Instead, he glared down the barrel of his pistol, said something Clint couldn't hear and steadied himself to fire.

Clint had been in enough scrapes to know when a man was bluffing and when he meant to pull the trigger. Whether he wanted to or not, a man that was going to fire tensed his legs and arm to get ready for the recoil of the gun in his hand. His eyes narrowed and his lips drew tight against his teeth.

Things like that were what turned a standoff into a gunfight. This time, however, it pulled a fourth man into the fray.

Still urging Eclipse to move forward, Clint leaned down over the stallion's neck, wrapped the reins around his left hand and drew his modified Colt with his right. In his mind, he could tell he had precious little time to act before that tall man took his shot that would either kill the man on the ground or the priest jumping in front of him.

Clint aimed as though the Colt was a part of his own

hand and he was simply pointing his finger at his target. From there, years of experience combined with a natural knack for marksmanship took over and he adjusted his aim in a fraction of a second.

He squeezed his trigger, felt the Colt buck against his hand and began swinging down from the saddle as Eclipse drew up next to the three men. Clint's bullet caught Eddie just behind his elbow, causing his gun hand to jerk upward as a reflexive response.

Eddie's pistol went off, but it sent its round into the air. As soon as he felt the pain from his own wound, Eddie pulled his arm in close to him, dropping his pistol in the process. He turned to see Eclipse riding straight for him and dropped down to retrieve his weapon, but he was too late to get ahold of it before he felt another impact, which caught him off-guard.

Swinging his leg over the saddle, Clint dropped down from Eclipse's back while keeping hold of both the reins and his pistol. His first boot landed squarely on the ground, while his other one caught Eddie on the shoulder. Clint didn't put much force behind his kick, but gave it just enough to push Eddie off-balance and away from the gun he'd dropped.

Tugging on the reins just enough to bring Eclipse to a stop, Clint held his Colt at the ready and said, "This has gone far enough."

For a moment, Eddie thought he'd been shot again and was falling because of it. When he nearly tripped and caught himself at the last moment, he realized that the dull ache on his back wasn't another bullet wound. He quickly looked at his elbow and saw that there was blood dripping from the injury there. He could move it just fine, however, despite a stinging, jabbing pain.

"Who the hell are you?" Eddie asked, bending his arm a couple times to work out the tensing muscles. "What's going on?"

The priest looked just as confused as he stood in front of Will with his arms held out and his eyes clenched shut. When he opened his eyes, the preacher positioned himself as though he now had to protect Will from both Eddie and Clint.

"Everybody just ease back," Clint said, while slowly holstering his Colt. "Take a breath and let's try to work out whatever set all of this into motion."

"Ease back?" Eddie asked, regaining some of his aggression. "You shot me!"

Clint shrugged. "It's just a nick."

Even though he'd been disarmed and nearly knocked off his feet, Eddie still had some fight in him. That much was obvious just by looking into his eyes. His gaze shifted quickly between Clint and Will as his brain churned through the possibility of still coming out of the situation a winner.

When he saw that he was less than three feet away from his pistol, Eddie took a breath and threw himself forward, lunging with both hands open. He had felt the touch of steel against one fingertip when he was suddenly stopped by something that he couldn't see.

Eddie came up short like a dog that had reached the end of its leash and spun around to find that Clint had grabbed hold of his collar. Suddenly furious, Eddie ripped himself out of Clint's grasp and started to reach one more time for the gun. He stopped again on his own when he saw Clint's hand flash to his Colt and hover there menacingly.

Keeping his hand less than an inch over his weapon, Clint said, "I'd keep real still if I was you."

FOUR

Eddie's face was flushed with anger and his hand trembled in anticipation. Although his gun was so very close, it seemed so far away. In all his life, he'd never seen someone move as fast as Clint had done. He thought again and again whether he could get ahold of his pistol before Clint drew his own.

Normally, Eddie would have taken the risk.

This time, he had to think twice.

That little bit of hesitation was all Clint needed. After taking one sideways step, he leaned down and swiped Eddie's gun up off the ground with a movement so fast that his arm looked like nothing but a blur. When he straightened up again, Clint had Eddie's gun in his right hand.

"Now, are we going to talk about this like men?" Clint asked. "Or would you rather have another go-around?"

Reluctantly, Eddie shook his head. He slapped away the hand Clint offered and stood up on his own.

Clint kept his smile cordial and took a step back to give the other man some breathing room. "Good to see it. Sorry about that little scratch," he said, pointing down to the bloody rip on Eddie's elbow. "A stitch or two should put you right back in the swing of things." Looking over to the priest, he asked, "You all right over there?"

The preacher was kneeling down next to Will, who was still crumpled on the ground. "I'm fine," he said in a somewhat shaky voice. "I'm not so sure about Will, though."

"I hope he dies." Eddie sneered. He looked as though he was about to walk over to Will, until he took a quick glance over toward Clint. The instant he saw the warning glare Clint was giving him, Eddie thought twice about what he was about to do and then decided to stay put. "What the hell do you care what I do?" he asked Clint. "Who the hell are you, anyways?"

"I'm someone who doesn't mind letting folks settle their own disputes," Clint answered. "But I'm also someone who doesn't take kindly to those who would shoot a priest or someone who's already down."

Eddie had sucked in a breath big enough to fuel the torrent of obscenities he was about to unleash when he noticed that Will wasn't exactly out of the fight just yet. His eyes widened when he saw the other man stirring on the ground and peeking up at him from over his shoulder.

"Son of a bitch," Eddie said. "That bastard ain't even dead."

Hearing that, Will twisted onto his back, before pulling his legs up underneath him. Not only wasn't he dead, but there wasn't even a spot of blood on his shirt, or anywhere else on his body for that matter. The only thing that even hurt on him was his left knee, since that had been the one to buckle when he'd stepped back and tripped on a raised board.

The preacher had been reaching out to help him and was now in the way as Will tried to get ahold of the gun that was tucked under his belt. He shoved the preacher aside with one arm and took a step back onto the leg that wasn't aching. From there, Will slapped his hand around the grip of his gun and pulled it free from where it had been kept.

Watching all of this unfold right in front of him, Clint could hardly believe his eyes. Just when he thought he'd defused the situation, someone comes running up with a burning match in his hand. Now, instead of worrying about what Eddie was going to do, Clint had to shift his focus onto the one person he thought wasn't a factor in the fight anymore.

Even more ironic was the fact that Eddie was now unarmed and was therefore the one in the most danger.

Clint let his reflexes take over as he stepped forward and reached out with one hand to grab hold of the barrel of Will's gun. He extended the other hand behind him to shove Eddie back and then twisted Will's gun with all the strength he could muster.

A wet cracking sound could be heard just before Will's face contorted painfully. The muscles in his arm were tensing reflexively, but his hand was twisted in such a way that his fingers couldn't have moved no matter what the rest of Will wanted to do.

When Clint had ridden into this, he'd made a decision not to hurt anyone unless it was absolutely necessary. Since he didn't know exactly who the men were and what they were fighting about, that seemed like a good decision at the time.

Now, however, Clint felt he was doing good in keeping himself from knocking both of those two into next week. He felt he'd probably broke at least one of Will's fingers just then, but he didn't feel bad about it in the least.

As soon as he felt no more resistance from Will, Clint pulled the gun from his hand and positioned himself so that he was standing sideways between the two combatants. From the corner of his eye, Clint could see Eddie lunging forward in yet another attempt to get his hands around the other man's throat.

Clint nipped that in the bud by hooking his hand around and back, clipping Eddie across the jaw with Will's gun. When he saw the smile growing on Will's face, Clint gave him a look as though he was going to knock it off with the same gun.

Angry, but not stupid, Will lowered his head and stepped back.

This time, rather than try to move on prematurely, Clint kept a tight grip on the gun he'd taken and snapped his foot back to kick Eddie's pistol even farther away. From there, he stepped back until he had his back to a wall and all three men in his line of sight.

"Thank you," the preacher said as he started to rush toward Clint. "Thank you so much."

Clint stopped the preacher with a quickly raised hand. "If you wouldn't mind just giving me a moment here before anyone makes any more sudden moves."

The preacher nodded and held out one open hand. "Would you like me to take that gun so we can settle this peacefully?"

"If it's all the same to you, I think I'll just keep hold of this," Clint replied. "I'll drop it off at the sheriff's office and be on my way."

"There's a problem with that," the preacher said hesitantly. "The law won't be through here for another couple days."

Clint rolled his eyes, wondering if he would ever learn that being a good Samaritan sometimes just didn't pay off. Of course, he didn't say that to the preacher. Instead, Clint tucked Will's gun under his belt next to his holster and put all three men behind him as he walked back to climb onto Eclipse's back.

FIVE

As soon as the show was over, the crowd that had gathered in the area drifted away. Clint had had enough of the entire thing and was feeling the last couple days' ride soak into his bones and aching muscles. Eddie and Will were out of steam as well and hobbled off in opposite directions to lick their wounds and bad-mouth each other from a safer distance.

After making sure the doctor was notified and that each man was in his place, the preacher jogged down the street in search of the newcomer who'd broken up the fight. There was no shortage of witnesses who'd watched the fireworks as well as the aftermath, so the preacher didn't have any problem learning where Clint had gone. The directions he got weren't precise, but for a town the size of Richwater, they were good enough.

The preacher walked quickly down one street and turned the corner onto another. From there, he kept his eyes open for the one thing that he figured would help point Clint out better than any other. Sure enough, after walking down another half a block, he spotted that exquisite Darley Arabian stallion that the stranger had been riding. The horse was tied up in front of the Gold Coast

Saloon, a place known more for its showgirls and nightly revues.

Stepping into the saloon, the preacher didn't have to look any farther than the closest end of the bar before he spotted the man he'd been looking for. Since the place was more of a night spot, the Gold Coast had a few hours before it hit its stride and was currently fairly empty. A few locals were scattered among a few tables, and one or two were nursing drinks at the bar.

Clint stood at the end of the bar with nobody on either side of him. By the look on his face, that was exactly the way he preferred it. Both his elbows were propped on top of the bar and a mug full of beer was in front of him. From where the preacher was standing, he could see that Clint's mouth was just curling into a smile.

That expression changed the instant Clint looked over and saw who had just walked through the front door.

Clint started to grumble, "Jesus Chr—" under his breath, but stopped when he reminded himself of who he was talking about. Trying to act as though he didn't even see the preacher, Clint turned his attention back to the cold brew he'd just gotten.

The foamy beer had just passed Clint's lips when he saw that the preacher was still in the saloon and headed in his direction. He took a moment to savor the taste of the beer before letting out a sigh and turning to look at the man in black, who'd taken the spot right next to him.

"If you want the gun I took," Clint said, "you can ask the bartender. I handed it over to him when I got here."

"Actually, I might let him keep it. I think it would be a better idea for Will to contemplate what happened in peace rather than with a weapon in his hand."

"And what about the other one?" As soon as he asked that question, Clint heard the familiar sound of steel pressing against flesh. He snapped his head around to look and found the preacher holding a very familiar pistol in the palm of his hand.

"This belongs to Eddie," the preacher said. "I picked it up when he wasn't looking. I think he assumes that someone stole it, but he didn't seem too upset by it when he was heading home. Would you like to keep this as well?"

"No," Clint answered. "But the bartender might. He seems to be getting quite a collection."

The preacher looked past Clint to a chubby man in his late thirties wearing an apron around his waist and his shirtsleeves rolled up to just below his elbows. He smiled when he saw the preacher holding out the gun as though he didn't even know what the handle was for.

"You look like you're afraid it'll bite ya, Father," the barkeep said. "Want me to take that off yer hands?"

Smiling, the preacher said, "I'd appreciate that, Sam. It belongs to Eddie. I hope it's not a bother to keep track of it for a little while."

"No problem at all. Mr. Adams here was right. I do have a bit of a collection. I figure it's better that I keep the guns back here with me than have them in the hands of some drunk. Most of 'em get so drunk that they forget where they left 'em and I don't remind 'em because they're probably gonna get liquored up again real soon."

"Not a bad community service," Clint said, lifting his mug. "Drunk's better than dead any day of the week."

The preacher smiled and handed over the weapon. When Sam asked him if he wanted a drink, he ordered a glass of water. All the while, he watched Clint with the eyes of someone well versed in reading the lines written upon others' faces.

"So your name is Adams?" the preacher finally asked.

At that moment, the barkeep returned with the glass of water. He set it down in front of the preacher and said, "Clint Adams, that's right. He's a known man, although you might not have heard about him."

Sam rocked back on his heels and looked over to Clint. All he got in return was a gaze frostier than the glass in the windowpanes which had been pummeled by the wintry cold. "All right, then," the barkeep said. "I'll let you two talk among yerselves."

The preacher waited until Sam had found something to do at the other end of the bar before looking to Clint and saying, "Funny thing that you'd introduce yourself to a bartender before sharing your name with me. I hope I didn't offend you back there, but it was a frightful situation."

"No offense taken," Clint said. "But one man was standing between two idiots waving guns around and another was offering me a beer. Which one would you be more friendly with?"

Smiling even wider, the preacher laughed a bit and took a sip of water. "You do have a point there. Perhaps I can make you feel more at ease. This really isn't a bad town and its people are good at heart. I'm Father Pryde."

Clint turned toward the preacher and shook his hand. "Clint Adams. Nice to meet you, Father."

"Welcome to Richwater."

SIX

After talking to Father Pryde for a couple minutes, Clint felt his nerves start to loosen up a bit and the ringing of gunshots fade from his ears. Conversation between him and the priest was easy and casual, sticking mostly to simple things like the weather and some local gossip. Before too long, Clint felt more at ease and even started to like talking to Pryde.

Of course, the beer Clint was drinking didn't hurt matters either.

Once he was relaxed enough to approach the topic again, Clint asked, "So what was going on between those two anyway? I hope I didn't step on any toes."

"Oh, I'd say you stepped on some toes all right. But they were toes that needed to be stepped on. Eddie has always been a hotheaded sort."

"What started the fight?"

"It's a story that's a little more involved than just a war of words. I'm sure you wouldn't be interested."

"I almost got myself shot, Father. That means I'm interested."

"Well, it all goes back to what drives most folks in this part of the country. Gold and the greed that accompanies it. I'm afraid that's something all too common for the types of men that travel to these parts. Plenty of souls come into and out of my parish, but most of them do so because they're chasing after a fortune of some kind. If it's not gold, it's silver. I even heard someone was after a diamond mine."

"Diamonds?" Clint said. "Really?"

"Oh yes. Of course, plenty of those tales are just that. Nothing but tales spread by bored miners and thieves trying to sell bogus maps and worthless claims."

Clint took another sip of beer and leaned back against the bar. "You'll find a lot of thieves wherever you go, Father. Unfortunately, they're not indigenous to gold country. I'm not a Bible scholar, but isn't money the root of all evil?"

"Ah yes," Pryde said, his face reflecting his enthusiasm for the turn the conversation had taken. "That's actually a bit of a misconception. The scripture actually says that the love of money is the root of all evil."

"I was close."

"Close, but there is a big difference, Mr. Adams. Money is nothing but folded paper and round bits of metal. It is the greed in men's hearts and the value they place on that metal and paper that gives rise to sin."

"I guess that makes sense. You must draw quite a crowd on Sundays."

"You should see for yourself. If you're still in town, I hope to see you at my service."

Suddenly, Clint felt a bit embarrassed. "You know something? I've been riding and working on my own schedule for so long that I'll be damned if I can think of what day it is. And before you give me a sermon on drinking, I haven't had anything but this one beer."

"It's all right. I remember how easily the days flow together when you spend enough time in the open country. In fact, town living is the only real excuse for naming the days of the week anyway."

"You sound like you spent a good amount of time on the trail."

"I used to bring the word of God to mining and railroad camps in my youth. Before that, I roamed and preached the Scriptures to those who were otherwise out of a normal priest's reach. Sometimes, I actually miss those days. Such freedom. Such a direct connection to the Almighty. I've been here for some many months now and appreciate where I am."

For a moment, Father Pryde drifted off into his own thoughts. He smiled and reflected as he took a sip of water and then finally brought himself back to the conversation. "Anyway, today is Friday. If you're still in Richwater on Sunday, I hope to see you. Miss Marple usually bakes a pie or two to be served afterward."

"Well, since there's going to be free dessert, how could I refuse?" Clint waited for a moment with a straight face until he saw the tight, forced smile on Father Pryde's face. "Just kidding, Father. Actually, it couldn't hurt for me to spend a little time in a church on Sunday. If I'm around, I'll be sure to drop by."

"I'm glad to hear that, Mr. Adams, I truly am. And a little surprised, if I may say so."

"Surprised?" Clint asked. "Why are you surprised?"

"Well, contrary to what Sam might think of me, I do get out of my church every so often. I've even had a life outside of the priesthood." Pryde paused for a moment and checked Clint's face just to make sure he wasn't about to speak out of turn. "I have heard of you, Mr. Adams. They call you The Gunsmith don't they?"

"Yes, they do."

"And it's not because you craft the weapons. It's because of your proficiency with them. Isn't that so?"

"Well, I do know the trade, Father. In fact, I still practice the craft every so often, but you're not all wrong in what you were saying. Folks do call me that, and most of them are talking about some of my more colorful experiences when they're saying what they say."

"You don't like being called that, do you?"

Clint looked over at the priest and studied him. Mostly, he noticed Pryde's eyes and that they were especially sharp. In fact, the man in black seemed to be sizing him up in much the same way that Clint might size up a man sitting across from him at a poker table. As something of an expert in those things himself, Clint recognized one of his own when he spotted him.

"It's not so much the name," Clint said. "But it's what comes with it that I don't care much for. People look at me differently when they find out who I am. Some of them seem afraid and others seem like they're waiting for a chance to gun me down."

"That's terrible," Pryde said.

"Sometimes. But other times, that name gets me a free drink or two from a barkeep who read about me in some trumped-up newspaper story." When he said that, Clint lifted his glass and nodded toward Sam. The barkeep returned the nod with a cordial wave and leaned in so he could whisper intently to the local he was serving.

"It seems like a trial being who you are," Pryde said. "If you'd prefer, I could refer to you by some other name."

"Nah, don't bother. Like it or not, it is my name and I'm not about to try to deny it. Thanks for the thought, though."

Clint finished his beer and watched as some more locals drifted in and out of the saloon. It seemed that the Gold Coast was more than just a place to buy liquor and watch a show. For Richwater, the saloon was a meeting place for young and old alike. Some folks came there for a quick cup of coffee before heading back out into the chilly day.

There were gray-haired women gathering at a table in front of a window playing hearts as well as a group of grizzled miners swapping bawdy jokes over shots of whiskey. It seemed there would even be some families coming in for dinner, since there was a sign advertising prices for daily specials.

But there was one local in particular that caught Clint's eye. She had smooth, olive-colored skin and luxurious dark brown hair that was pulled back into a single braid which fell down just past her shoulders. Her lips were the color of ripe cherries and looked full and soft. Her whole face seemed to glow when she looked over toward Clint and smiled.

For a moment, Clint thought he'd just won a jackpot. Then he saw her wave and head in his direction.

"Hello, Father Pryde," she said. "I don't see you in here too often."

So Clint hadn't won the jackpot, but the game was far from over.

SEVEN

The priest's face lit up as well when he saw the brunette walk through the door and smile at him. He stood up at attention, his smile brightening the closer she got.

Looking over at him, Clint smirked and nudged Pryde with his elbow. "Still got some life in ya, huh, Father?"

Responding in a whisper, Father Pryde said, "I may be ordained, but I'm not dead."

The priest quickly stopped his whispering once the brunette was close enough to hear. She walked up to him and made a show of leaning over to check the glass he was holding.

"I hope that's nothing too strong, Father," she said.

"There's no sin against a man imbibing every now and then," Pryde said. "Besides, this is only water."

Clint couldn't keep himself from letting his eyes wander up and down the brunette's body once she got so close to him. She was wearing a pink dress with thin ribbons sewn into the fabric. It was conservatively cut, but still tight enough to showcase her figure. Her waist formed a nice, gentle hourglass shape, curving up into firm, rounded breasts.

"Clint Adams," Pryde said, suddenly drawing the brunette's attention toward him, before Clint could get his eyes away from where they'd been lingering. "I'd like to introduce you to Josie Moynahan."

When Clint looked up, he saw that Josie was already staring at him. Going by the look on her face, she knew that he'd been studying her figure, but didn't seem too offended by it. Giving him a sly, knowing smirk, she extended a hand and said, "Pleased to meet you."

"And you," Clint said, trying to keep from looking too flustered. "I was just, ahhh, admiring your dress."

"Really? And what about the bow? Do you like the color?"

"Yes I do. It looks very—"

"There is no bow, Mr. Adams."

"Well, I guess that will teach me to not lie to such an observant woman," Clint said with a guilty shrug. "Sometimes a man just can't keep his eye from admiring true beauty. Just like he sometimes can't keep his mouth from laying it on a bit thick."

Josie smiled at that and seemed to relax. "At least your heart's in the right place. It is nice to meet you." This time when she said that, she seemed to truly mean it. She let her own eyes linger on Clint for a moment before turning back to Pryde. "I heard gunshots earlier today. Word is there was some kind of fight and that you were mixed up in it, Father. I hope it was nothing serious."

"Will Ambrose and Eddie were at each other's throats again," the priest replied. "It turned out all right, but that's mainly because of Mr. Adams, here. Things would have gotten a lot worse if he hadn't happened by."

Josie looked back over to Clint and gave him another warm smile. "Really? I'd love to hear about that. It would be the most exciting thing that's happened here in a while."

"I'd be happy to tell you about it," Clint said. "Perhaps over dinner?"

"I'm not sure about that."

"Oh, you'll love it. I even promise to make up plenty of juicy details which will make me look like something out of an adventure novel."

She started to laugh, but then nodded and said, "Well, if you put it that way, I don't see a reason to refuse. I love a good story."

"Doesn't everyone? I am new in town, though, so you'll have to pick a good place to eat."

"Here's as good a place as any," she said. "I'll meet you back here for dinner. Father Pryde, it was nice running into you. I've got to have a word with Sam and then I've got some errands to run."

"Then be quick about it," Pryde said. "I wouldn't want to keep you long."

Josie gave them both a quick wave and walked on down the bar, where Sam was waiting. Acting completely on impulse, Clint watched her leave with an approving eye. The way she let her hips sway back and forth as she moved, Josie knew damn well that she had an appreciative audience.

When Clint had had his fill for the moment, he turned around to get his beer and discovered that Father Pryde hadn't quite gotten his eyeful just yet. Clint sipped his beer and laughed under his breath.

"Alive and kicking, huh, Father?" he said jokingly.

The priest cleared his throat and acted as though he'd really been staring at something else in that same part of the room. "Of course, of course. No harm done."

"None at all."

"So do you think you will be staying on until Sunday?"

"Don't worry yourself so much," Clint said. "I'm about due for a few nights with a roof over my head, and I'll be sure not to miss your sermon."

Father Pryde shook his head as the humor drained from his face. "That's not why I asked."

Seeing the change that had come over the other man, Clint leaned with his hip against the bar so he could face Pryde when he spoke again. "What's the problem then? You look like someone just walked over your grave."

"Not mine, but there may be a fresh grave around here soon enough, I'm afraid."

"Are you talking about those two morons that were tangling earlier?"

"Eddie and Will, yes. I'm afraid Eddie is the vengeful type and will bring harm to poor Will sooner rather than later."

"From what I heard, they both had a bit of blame in the matter. Didn't Will steal something from the other one?"

"Perhaps, but that is no reason for violence."

"No, but it is a reason to tell the sheriff." As soon as he said that, Clint winced and remembered why that wasn't possible. "Or at least tell whoever acts as the law when the sheriff is away. I'm a visitor here, Father. Just passing through."

"Could you have a talk with Eddie? That's all I'm asking." Pausing, Father Pryde leaned forward and gave Clint a mischievous wink. "I'll put in a good word for you with Josie."

Clint looked over to where the brunette was standing. As if on cue, she leaned over the bar to pick something off of Sam's shirt. The action caused her back to curve in just a way so that her rounded backside was magnificently highlighted.

"The things a man will do for a pretty face," Clint grumbled.

"You're a good man, Mr. Adams. I'm sure a little talk from someone like you would be enough to set Eddie on the right path. He's a good man, but a little quick to let his temper flare."

"Tell me something, Father. If I put a real good scare

into him, will you pay for my dinner, too?"

Pryde started to answer, but cut himself short and laughed a bit uncomfortably.

The one thing that Clint couldn't help but notice was that the priest actually seemed to consider the offer for a moment. His light brown hair had fallen just enough in front of his face that it covered a good portion of his eyes. Because of that, Clint couldn't be sure if he'd really seen that glimpse of indecision or not.

Whether or not it had been there at all, it was gone now, and Pryde shrugged amiably. "This town is my flock, Mr. Adams. Without a sheriff around, I need to look out for my flock's best interests."

"Can't blame you for that," Clint said. "Where can I find Eddie?"

EIGHT

Clint took his time finishing his beer and listened to what more the priest had to say. Father Pryde seemed only too anxious to lay out the rest of what had happened once Clint had ridden away from the fight he'd stopped. Now that Clint had an idea of what to look for, he noticed a couple things about what came out of Pryde's mouth.

First of all, there wasn't a single thing in there to make Eddie look like anything but a foul-mouthed bully. Even though Clint didn't know either one of the men from Adam, he'd seen all of them at a moment when the furthest thing from their minds was keeping up appearances.

If times of stress were good for anything, it was getting straight down to the core of a man. Everything came to the surface, from cowardice to heroism, and even lies were harder to tell once the bullets started to fly. Clint might not have seen much, but neither Eddie nor Will struck him as being particularly wicked men.

Pissed off, definitely. Just not bad at heart.

The other thing Clint noticed wasn't anything too hard to spot, but it stuck out to him all the same. Father Pryde was very anxious for Clint to not only stay in town, but possibly take over the sheriff's position as well. The priest hadn't said that in so many words, but Pryde couldn't stress enough how much his flock needed tending and how a man of Clint's "obvious talents" was so suited for the job.

Clint soaked all of this up as he listened to Father Pryde tell his story and give the directions needed to catch up with Eddie Vale. Once he was finished, Pryde set a few coins onto the bar to cover the price of Clint's beer.

"It's the least I can do," Pryde said with a smile. And with that, he headed for the front door.

Waiting until the priest was long gone, Clint motioned for Sam to come back over.

The barkeep spotted the money laying on the bar the way a hawk would spot a mouse running in an open stretch of field. Pouncing on the coins and stashing them in his pocket, Sam swept up Pryde's glass and looked over to Clint. "Can I get you another?"

"Not just yet," Clint replied, shaking his head. "But I was wondering if you'd heard about what happened earlier today. You know, the run-in between—"

"Oh yes," Sam interrupted. "Eddie and Will going at it again. You'd be hard-pressed to find someone around here who didn't know by now. If that damn sheriff of ours could drop in on us sooner, we wouldn't have dust-ups like that."

"So those two go around like that a lot?"

"Sure they do. But men always get their blood boiling when there's so much at stake."

Now Clint could feel his interest truly growing. Having one of the coldest poker faces in the game, however, he found it no problem keeping his thoughts to himself. "There's a lot at stake?" Clint asked in a voice mixed with just the right amount of apathy.

If there was one thing any bartender loved, it was gossip. When there were no girls on stage or a man playing piano, the barkeep's stories were some of the best entertainment in a saloon. Clint played on that perfectly by acting as though, with the arrival of this new topic, he was suddenly thinking twice about leaving.

"There's plenty at stake," Sam said. "At least, most folks around here would consider a vein of gold longer than this bar to be plenty."

This time, not only did Clint let his interest show, but he accentuated it just enough to let Sam know he'd been hooked. "Damn, that is a hell of a lot of gold. Are you sure that's not just some tall miner's tale?"

"Anywhere else, and I might think so myself. But in this neck of the woods, we take stories about gold real seriously. It's how plenty of us make out living, after all. It's how I paid for this saloon."

"Is that a fact?"

"Yessir," Sam said proudly. "Made a nice little strike a few years ago and went into business for myself. I came out of it a lot better than some. The problem most fellas have is that they don't know when to quit scroungin' and when to find something else to do with their time."

"So this rumor going around about this vein of gold," Clint said, carefully steering the conversation back to where he wanted it without looking too anxious to get there, "what's that got to do with those two that were fighting?"

The barkeep looked a little hesitant to go on, until Clint offhandedly motioned to his beer mug. After refilling the drink, Sam decided he wasn't losing anything by spending so much time bending Clint's ear. "Now the only reason I know this," Sam said, after leaning down and propping one elbow onto the bar, "is because I heard Will Ambrose himself talking about it no less than two days ago.

"Will had had a bit too much to drink and was getting a little loose around the lips, if you know what I mean. Anyway, he says that he heard about this vein of gold waiting to be dug up and I told him that everyone in town has heard of it. That's when he says that he knows more than the stories. He says he's got a map."

"A map?" Clint said. "Now this is clearing up a bit."

Sam nodded and took a quick glance around to make sure nobody was listening in. He did that mainly to add drama to his own story, since the closest person to them was a gray-haired mountain man who had his face buried in a bowl of stew. "He said he didn't have the map just yet, but was expectin' it real soon. Wouldn't you know it, but Eddie comes in later that same night and tells pretty much the same story."

"He said he was getting a map, too?"

Sam nodded again, relishing the fact that Clint seemed so wrapped up in his story. "Next day comes, both of 'em sober up, and there's no more word about any map. But Eddie starts buying drinks for the whole place and Will looks like someone shot his best friend. Day after that, they're at each other's throat. You figure out the rest."

Seeing that the barkeep's story was over, Clint shrugged and sipped his beer. "That's a hell of a thing. I wonder if there really is a map."

"Who can say? I'd bet there's something, though; otherwise there wouldn't be so many ruffled feathers around here."

For a moment, Clint thought it over. Then he shook his head and took a healthy pull from his mug. "Eh, who cares? Map or not, I won't see any of that gold. There probably isn't any gold anyway."

"Yeah, you could be right." For a moment, Sam stood by as though he was waiting for Clint to tell him that he'd been kidding or that he wanted to hear more about the fabled strike that had yet to be found. But he couldn't read much past the unconcerned facade that Clint had up. Hell, there were some professional gamblers who couldn't see through that well-practiced mask.

"I guess it could all be a story," Sam finally concluded.

"Maybe it's like I said before. Folks around here get pretty wrapped up in gold tales. Might seem silly to someone who's not from around here."

"Not silly," Clint said, allowing the corner of his mouth to curl a little. "Just a little hard to swallow. Probably because I'm not from around here, just like you said."

Now Sam was beginning to feel like he was no longer being taken seriously. But Clint was careful to seem skeptical rather than condescending, and he'd done a good job. The barkeep simply straightened up and figured his audience was no longer interested.

"Well, if you want to hear any more good stories about us crazy miners, just let me know. Father Pryde still can't get enough of them after a month of letting me prattle on for hours at a time." Sam said.

"He's taken an interest lately, too, has he?"

"Well, yes. But he's only been here that long."

That struck a nerve in the back of Clint's mind, which the barkeep didn't seem to notice. Instead, the other man was looking around at his other customers and getting a few impatient waves in return.

"I've got some glasses to fill," Sam said, already moving away.

"Thanks a lot, Sam. I'll be seeing you later." When Clint got up, he dropped enough money onto the bar to cover his drinks plus a little to keep on Sam's good side. And even though he left the place looking like he'd already forgotten the rumors he'd heard, Clint's mind was going over them again and again.

By the time he was outside the Gold Coast, Clint was already coming up with questions of his own. Those questions alone were enough to make him forget about the thought of getting some sleep and moving on in the morning. Sure, it would have been easier to let Richwater solve its own problems, but the easy trail never had the best scenery.

Although it sometimes got him into trouble, Clint rarely tried to fight his sense of curiosity. That was the part of him that led him to the most interesting trails of all. And when there were men in dispute over something like a possible fortune in gold, things tended to get real interesting real quick.

Then again, perhaps being in gold country did have an effect on him. He could ride a hell of a long way with some of that gold in his saddlebags.

NINE

The first place Clint checked to find Eddie was the doctor's office. In Richwater, the doctor and dentist, as well as a lawyer, all conducted business in the same building. Not too surprisingly, the lawyer took up two of the rooms within the building's two floors, while each doctor only got one. No doubt, the doctors were talked out of the extra space moments before signing the lease.

It was a squat little building nestled between a land surveyor's office and a dressmaker's shop. The moment Clint stepped inside, he could smell the bitter scent of various ointments and bandages that reminded him of every other doctor's office he'd ever visited. There was another more pungent scent that caught Clint's attention, which he figured probably came from the lawyer's office upstairs.

According to Father Pryde, the man Clint needed to see was Dr. James. Clint found him without any trouble since the portly physician was right through the door that was marked with his name. When Clint asked about where he might find Eddie Vale, all he got was a nod and three grunted words in response.

"Sent him home." That said, the doctor went back to

whatever he was doing at his little desk and pretended that Clint had already left.

"Could you tell me where that is?" Clint asked.

This time when the doctor looked up, he focused his eyes on Clint's face and studied him for a moment. "You a friend or relative?"

"I'm his cousin," Clint answered, deciding to try and take a short route through the questions that might be in his future.

Sure enough, after pondering for all of two seconds, Dr. James shrugged his sloping shoulders and rattled off a quick set of directions through thick, blubbery lips. Once he was done, he blinked and went back to his paperwork.

"Much obliged," Clint said with a tip of his hat.

The doctor didn't even look up this time, but merely waved and shifted in his seat.

Clint was only too glad to put the smells behind him and leave the building. According to the doctor, Eddie lived somewhere on the other side of town, about four blocks away. Of course, since Richwater was small by anyone's standards, that translated to about five minutes of walking time, which Clint stretched into seven just to enjoy the fresh air.

He arrived at the area Dr. James had mentioned and found a cluster of four small homes all in a row. Starting at one end, Clint looked at each in turn before picking one as the most likely prospect. It helped that it was the only house that appeared to have any signs of life coming from inside.

Clint stepped up to the door, knocked a few times and then stepped to one side. If this was Eddie's home and he took a peek through the door, he might not be too happy to see Clint waiting there on the other side.

Sounds of footsteps could be heard coming from inside and then stopped at the door. There was some rustling back and forth as whoever was there tried to look through the window and possibly through the crack between door and jamb.

Finally, a muffled voice asked, "Who is it?"

"Is that you, Eddie?" Clint asked, speaking clearly and calmly, which was plenty different than the last time he'd spoken to the man.

"Yeah. What do you want?"

"Father Pryde sent me."

There was a bit of a pause, a loud, grumbling sigh, and then the door was opened. Clint waited until he saw Eddie stick his nose out from inside the house, and he braced himself for a wide range of possibilities that might follow.

Eddie looked out, turned his head one way and then turned it the correct way so that he could finally see who was there. When he saw Clint, his eyes widened and he spat out a snarling curse before darting back inside and slamming the door shut.

Clint was just fast enough to snap one foot out and through the opening before the door was closed all the way. Of course, that also meant that he was just fast enough to feel that same door pound against the side of his boot and send a crushing pain all the way up his leg.

Trying to keep himself calm, Clint stepped forward so he could see through the gap he'd created. "I just want to talk to you, Eddie. Father Pryde really did send me."

"Get off my property before I shoot you."

"With what?" Clint asked, gambling that a simple miner wouldn't have more than one firearm. "Father Pryde took your pistol. I know because he came to me with it."

The more time that passed, the more Clint's mind became filled with images of Eddie walking over to a rack and pulling down some hunting rifle which would have no problem blasting through a wooden door. "I don't have to come in," Clint said. "I can talk to you right here, but it would help if you opened the door at least."

A few moments went by and Clint could see Eddie standing there idly on the other side of the door.

"I'll even step back if you want," Clint offered.

"How do I know you won't shoot me?" Eddie asked. "Someone told me about you. They said you was a gunfighter. They said you killed more men than the pox."

Clint rolled his eyes and laughed slightly. "That's one I haven't heard before."

"You took a shot at me already!" Eddie said, his voice filling with renewed energy. "How do I know you won't kill me now?"

Peeking through the door he kept wedged open, Clint could see that Eddie was nervously stepping closer. "If I wanted to kill you so badly, why wouldn't I have done it earlier?"

"I don't know," Eddie replied hesitantly.

"What if I told you I knew about the map?"

When he heard that, Eddie didn't know whether to open the door or try even harder to push it shut.

TEN

Even a town as small as Richwater got its fair share of visitors. That was mainly due to the fact that it had been built along a well-worn trail used by miners, traders and travelers alike. Because of this, folks didn't take much notice of a new face as it pulled into town. That is, not unless that new face had kicked up as much commotion as Clint had upon his arrival.

By the time Kyle Hammund made it into Richwater's borders, the locals were occupied with spreading rumors and gossip concerning the morning's scuffle and the appearance of The Gunsmith. That was all fine and good as far as Hammund was concerned. Not only was he accustomed to traveling without folks noticing, but it was an important requirement in his line of work.

He rode into town alone, atop a light gray horse with dark spots on its flanks. His wide-brimmed hat was tilted down to cover the upper half of his face, and his cold, dark eyes stared out from under it like two polished chunks of obsidian. Dark brown hair hung down from the hat in dirty strands. His narrow build, combined with the strawlike appearance of his hair, made him look even more like a scarecrow that had found a way down from its post.

He rode in a straight line through town, ignoring the occasional looks he would get from people on either side of the street. Even those that did notice him didn't pay him any mind. They could tell with a glance that the man on the pale horse was definitely not interested in shooting the breeze.

In fact, the only thing that brought those few locals' eyes to him in the first place was the occasional sparkle that would come from his hip. Kept there in a finely crafted, customized holster was a pistol that could just barely be seen since it was held down by crossing straps which buckled the gun in place. The weapon was covered and secured so tightly because its handle was plated in gold and there were even traces of gold running along its barrel.

Normally, it would take a keen eye to spot the gold underneath all of that leather, but Richwater was in gold country and many locals there made their living by being able to spot the slightest trace of the precious metal. It was some of the older folks in town who spotted the dull gleam at Hammund's side. They looked away even quicker when they saw the intense glare in Kyle's eyes.

Gold might be valuable, but so was the ability to know when something was too much trouble to think about. Paying the gold at Hammund's side a second thought was just as smart as digging in a deep shaft when the rock ceiling was already shaking over your head. The few people who'd noticed the gun turned away and went about their business, allowing Hammund to ride on.

Kyle noticed the ones who'd looked his way. In the space of a few seconds, he sized each of them up and didn't figure any of them were worth another glance either. Instead, he kept riding until he got to a small feed store at the end of a street, next to the Richwater telegraph office. He tied the light gray horse to the closest post and stepped onto the boards laying along that side of the street.

His long black duster covered almost his entire body, and Kyle made sure to pull it shut over his holster. Pulling open the door, he stepped into the feed store and stood there for a moment to take a look at who was inside the place.

There wasn't much of anyone except for one man in his early twenties picking up a sack of chicken feed. He hefted the sack over one shoulder and turned around to glance at a man a couple years his senior standing behind a short counter.

"Don't get up or nothing, Matt," the young man said. "I can carry this out on my own."

"If you couldn't, you're gonna need a lot more than that to get your farm earning money," the man behind the counter replied.

Suddenly, the younger man seemed to get real uncomfortable and it didn't have anything to do with the weight he was carrying. "Yeah, about that. You think I could pay you for this once I see some profit? Times are hard especially with me starting over and all."

The man behind the counter paused as he strained to get a look at who'd just entered his shop. He looked down the row of barrels and premeasured bags of corn and grain to see Kyle Hammund's tall form taking up a good portion of the front doorway. "That'll be fine," Matt said. "Pay me when you can. I think I might be seeing some profit of my own real soon."

Smiling and letting out a relieved sigh, the young farmer picked up his pace toward the front door. "You're a good man, Matt. I'll pay you back with interest as soon as I can manage it."

Kyle stepped into the store and held open the door so the farmer could walk past him. Once the younger man was out, Kyle locked the door and walked up to the counter, where Matt was waiting. Hammund's dark eyes remained fixed on the store owner and each of his steps sounded like rocks being dropped onto the worn planks of the floor.

Finally, Hammund made it to the front, where he stopped and glowered silently down at the other man. "Anyone in back?" he asked.

First, Matt shook his head and then he followed up with a quick "No. Nobody's here."

"You get the telegram I sent?"

"Yep. I sure did. Everything you asked for is in the back and bundled up for you. Want me to get it?"

Kyle nodded once, which was enough to get Matt out from behind the counter and into the back room. He followed the store owner with his eyes, keeping the rest of his body perfectly still. Even when Matt was gone for longer than it should have taken to fetch the supplies he was holding, Kyle didn't move.

Kyle didn't move when he heard the sounds of more than one set of footsteps heading his way from that same back room.

He did move when he saw Matt return not only with a large box filled with digging and camping supplies but with three men behind him. Each of the three men looked old enough to have used the guns they were carrying, but not by much.

"You gonna be a good man and hand over that box without a fuss?" Kyle asked.

Matt took one look over his shoulder as all three men raised their pistols. He then turned back to face Kyle and said, "Not this time."

ELEVEN

"This isn't smart, Matt," Kyle said while taking a step back from the counter, so he was looking straight ahead at all four men. "Not even for you."

Certain that he had his backup in place, the store owner walked up to the counter and set the box down roughly. All the supplies inside jumbled and shifted. The impact made a resounding thump, which echoed throughout the store. "You know what's not smart?" Matt said. "Letting someone like you walk into my store and boss me around."

Kyle's voice remained even and steady. The first hint of strain couldn't be heard when he said, "All you had to do was keep an eye on who came and left this town, gather these things and have them ready for me when I got here. Where do those three fit in?"

"They fit in because they're the ones who'll see you out. Out of my store, out of my sight and out of my town." Matt took a deep breath and committed himself to his decision. "You've got till the count of five and I swear we're done. I won't even tell the law about this."

"What law?" Kyle asked. "There hasn't been a badge in this piss hole for weeks. Maybe months."

By this time, the three gunmen had stepped forward and moved in front of Matt. One of them wore a dark blue bandanna around a thick, pale neck. The second was a bald man with a clean shaven face. The third was a Mexican with a mustache that was thick enough to cover the entire lower half of his face.

The man with the bandanna stood in front of the counter. The bald one stepped out into the aisle, next to a stack of feed sacks, and the Mexican kept moving sideways until the edge of his foot bumped against a barrel filled with corn. Between the three of them, they had the entire store covered.

There was nowhere for Kyle to go without being in at least two of the gunmen's sights. Even with all of that under consideration, Kyle didn't seem overly concerned. In fact, he hadn't moved since he'd readjusted his stance to look at all of the men head-on.

The store had gotten so quiet once the three gunmen found their spots that the sounds of people talking and moving about outside the store filled every man's ears. Matt felt his heart pound in his chest and a cold sweat break out on his forehead. When he pulled in a breath, he could feel every muscle involved straining with the effort.

When he spoke, Matt's voice sounded like a crack of thunder. "One."

Kyle snapped his coat open with a flick of his wrist, causing the edge of material to catch on the handle of his pistol. In the same fluid motion, he flipped his thumb to release the straps holding the gun inside its holster.

"Two," Matt uttered with a slight waver in his voice.

All three of the other gunmen had their eyes focused on Kyle. Their grips tightened around their weapons and every one of their senses tuned in to the moment.

"Thr—"

"Five," Kyle interrupted as his hand flashed down to pluck the gold-plated firearm from where it hung at his side. The pistol was a .45 and looked big enough to be cumbersome in anyone's hand. But as soon as Kyle wrapped his fingers around its handle, the gun seemed to leap out of its leather and spit out flashes of sparks and white smoke.

That first bullet whipped through the air and punched a hole through the chin of the man wearing the bandanna. Several more bullets followed soon after as all three of Matt's gunmen squeezed their triggers when panic began to tighten its fingers around their hearts.

The man wearing the bandanna got one shot off only because his finger tensed around his trigger out of reflex. Pain flooded through every inch of him as hot lead tore a path through his lower jaw and out the other side. The back of his head exploded with a shower of blood, bone and teeth as the rest of his body slammed back against the counter.

The bald shooter and the Mexican fired pretty much at the same time, but their shots were hurried and missed Kyle by a few inches. By the time they'd gotten some of their wits about them, their target had almost halved in size as Kyle dropped to one knee and pulled his head down low.

From his new stance, Kyle extended his gun arm and sighted down the barrel. He took his time and sent a bullet into the Mexican's chest since that was the hardest target for him to see. When he saw that man jerk back and let out a pained grunt, Kyle turned to aim at the bald man as another pair of shots hissed over his head.

The bald man had taken a shot at where Kyle's head should have been, squeezing off a round before he could readjust his aim. He could hear the Mexican grunting in pain as he staggered back against the barrels, but tried to put that sound out of his mind. What weighed on him even heavier was the putrid smell of death coming from the spot in front of the counter.

Fighting back the shakes that were overtaking his body, the bald gunman kept firing. He pulled his hand down toward the middle of Kyle's crouching body, but then he couldn't get his hand to stop. It was as though his entire arm had fallen asleep and simply hung like a wet noodle from his shoulder.

The bald man felt something heavy drag past his leg, followed by an impact on top of his boot. Looking down, he saw that the heavy object had been his own pistol, which had slipped from his hand. Before he could think too long about how his gun had gotten away from him, he realized he was going blind as well.

That's when he felt the pinch in his heart, followed by the wave of hot, and then that went numb as well. He was dead before he hit the floor, two fresh holes drilled through his chest just left of center.

When he saw the bald man drop his gun and fall over, Kyle got back onto both feet and casually made his way down the aisle. He kept his eyes on the last spot he'd seen the Mexican, but watched Matt from the corner of his field of vision.

Kyle stepped over a short stack of empty sacks and looked down at where the Mexican had landed. Although shot in the chest, the Mexican was still alive and fighting to pull in a breath. He held his gun in hand, but didn't have enough strength left to keep it when Kyle delivered a short kick, which sent the pistol skidding across the floor.

Once again, silence descended upon the smoke-filled air, only to be broken by the Mexican's labored wheezing. Kyle stood as though he was carved from stone, watching with vague interest as the Mexican hacked up a mouthful of pink foam.

Kyle could tell just by looking at him that the Mexican had been shot through the lungs. That telltale foam slid down the man's chin as his breathing became more and more strained. When the Mexican got the strength to look up, Kyle put a round right between his eyes and then headed back toward the counter.

For a moment, he couldn't see any trace of Matt. There wasn't a sound to be heard, and the only thing moving that Kyle could see was the acrid smoke that swirled through the air. He grinned to himself while moving around the counter and looked down at the figure he knew he'd find cowering there.

Matt simply didn't have anyplace else to go.

Seeing that he'd been discovered, Matt spun around so quickly that he fell onto his back. He started to sputter some words in his defense, but couldn't get out anything intelligible.

Kyle didn't bother trying to decipher the other man's babbling. Instead, he shook his head, lifted his gun and said, "Matt, my good man, it looks like you picked the wrong day to take a stand."

TWELVE

The door swung open just as Clint was beginning to think he wasn't getting in. Eddie held on to the handle as though he was just waiting for the right moment to slam it in Clint's face. But rather than do anything so dramatic, he kept his distance and let Clint into his home. Clint noticed that the door wasn't shut completely behind him. Perhaps Eddie was preparing for a quick getaway.

Looking around the sparsely furnished home, Clint tried not to make any sudden moves, since Eddie seemed jumpy enough already. Instead, he kept his hands where they could be seen and let his eyes wander from one side of the living space to another.

There wasn't much to see. Apart from a couple broken-down chairs, a table filled with clutter and a little dirty stove, Eddie only had his clothes laying about the house. It took Clint a second glance to realize that one particularly big stack of laundry was actually a few clothes piled on top of a bed. The place smelled like old food, but at least there wasn't anywhere for anyone else to hide.

"Nice place you have here, Eddie," Clint said.

The thin, balding man edged away from the door, walking in a crablike sideways shuffle. He was obviously moving toward a holster that was hanging over the back of a chair, but Clint didn't concern himself with that, since he could see the holster was empty.

"It keeps the rain out," Eddie replied. "What do you want?"

"Like I said, Father Pryde asked me to come over here and have a talk with you."

"He make you the acting sheriff?"

"No."

"Then I don't have to talk to you."

Nodding, Clint said, "That's true, but at least let me try. I mean, you wouldn't want me to shirk on a job given to me by a priest, would you?"

Eddie wasn't at all taken in by Clint's pleasant tone or his easy manner. In fact, his muscles tensed and he backed toward the stove. "You said you knew about the map. What do you know about it?"

"Mind if I sit down?"

Once Eddie shook his head, Clint stepped over to the closest chair and lowered himself onto it. Despite the fact that it felt as though the legs might snap from under him, the chair was actually quite comfortable. Then again, it was one of the few times Clint had been off his feet all day. Besides giving his body a break, Clint thought Eddie might be more relaxed as well if he saw that Clint wasn't completely mobile. Sure enough, as soon as Clint let out a relaxed sigh, Eddie seemed to let his guard down a bit.

Clint picked up on that instantly and adjusted his mannerisms to make Eddie feel more at ease. "First of all, I apologize for giving you that little scrape earlier."

"You shot me," Eddie said, pointing toward the single strip of bandage looped around his arm.

"Well, I apologize. All I wanted to do was step in and lend a hand before someone got killed."

"That thieving bastard deserves to get killed for what he done! I shoulda put a bullet through Will's head the moment I found out he took what was mine."

"You mean the map," Clint said for clarification.

"You're damn right I mean the map. What the hell else would I mean? And that damn . . ." Eddie trailed off just then. It didn't seem so much that he was afraid of what Clint might do, but more like something inside him just took hold of his tongue and wouldn't let go.

Just like in a card game, Clint recognized this as the best moment to make his move. Everything else had just been leading up to that one instant. Even though he wasn't certain he would get what he wanted, Clint knew this was the best time to make his play. After all, that's why they called it gambling.

"You were going to say 'that damned preacher,' weren't you?" Clint asked, doing an excellent job of keeping his tone neutral and free of accusation.

Eddie's nostrils flared and he pulled in a deep breath. Then he nodded and straightened himself up to his full height for the first time since Clint had come into his home. "What if I was? Are you gonna run back and tell him so he can damn my soul to hell?"

Holding up his hands, Clint shook his head. "Not at all. You see, the good father may have asked me to come here, but that doesn't mean I'm his errand boy. Actually, I was going to come here on my own, but Pryde had to step in and start giving orders like he runs this town."

"I'll bet he did," Eddie said, nodding and buying into Clint's annoyed tone just like Clint thought he would.

Not letting on that he noticed the lessening of tension within the house, Clint said, "Here I tried to lend a hand and settle a fight and all I get is some preacher ordering me about for my troubles. The least he could have done was pay for my meal or something."

"That'd be the day," Eddie said as he pulled up a chair for himself and sat down. "I'd like to know if'n he ever spends any of the donations he gets from the widows and old folks around here. He's the first to pass that plate around, but I ain't never seen so much as one new hymnal. Hell, the first-row pew is still nearly cracked in two."

"Is that a fact?"

"It sure is."

For the first time since he'd gotten there, Clint didn't think that Eddie was about to jump out the nearest window at the first chance he got.

"And I'll bet he's been that way ever since he got here, which was about three, four years ago, I bet?"

Eddie looked at Clint and shook his head. "It's only been a month, but damn, it sure feels longer."

That settled one discrepancy that had been nagging at Clint's mind, but he barely flinched before moving on to another subject. "And in all that time, I bet he's taken men like Will Ambrose under his wing."

Eddie's face twisted into a scowl. "He sure has."

"And what does Pryde think Will's going to do now that he has the map to himself? He's probably after him for a fat donation after stepping in on his behalf."

"You see a lot for an outsider," Eddie said. "Wish I could say I thought of that much on my own."

"Sometimes it takes someone not involved in something to see everything that's going on. Kind of like a neighbor settling a dispute between family members."

"I guess, but I don't take kindly to being called Will's family."

If Clint had been playing cards with Eddie right then, he would have sat back and started planning on how to spend his winnings. Not only did he feel that he'd gotten into the other man's confidence, but Clint thought he might have even gained a higher spot in Eddie's mind than folks the balding man had known for years. It was a tenuous situation, though, and one that could be shattered with one overly confident move.

"Pryde asked if I might stand in for the law since the

sheriff's out of town, and I just might do that after all," Clint said. "It seems things aren't quite balanced here and Pryde may be trying to pick sides."

Eddie seemed wrapped up in his own gripes, however, and said, "You know, that preacher never once came to me and asked if he could help. But at least Will won't be getting rich just yet."

"He's got the map, hasn't he?"

"Yeah, but only half."

"Half?" Clint asked, trying not to sound as shocked as he felt.

"Yeah. The other half's supposed to arrive sometime soon." Grinning, Eddie added, "I'll bet that damn preacher didn't tell you that, did he?"

THIRTEEN

Although Eddie seemed more than willing to shoot the breeze with Clint until he ran out of wind, the balding man didn't really have any new information to give. Either that, or he was guarding it much better than Clint expected. Either way, Clint excused himself after a few more minutes and left Eddie to stew once again on his own.

Clint had the feeling that he'd been steered toward Eddie as if he was going to finish the man off in his own home at the first sign of trouble. Actually, if Clint hadn't worked so hard to ease the other man's nerves, Eddie might very well have tried something that would have sparked another fight.

But Clint didn't go into that house expecting to bully Eddie into admitting fault or into promising to keep away from Will. On the contrary, Clint had gone in wanting to hear the other side of the story concerning this map that had been the topic of so much discussion.

All the while, Clint had been wondering how come nobody else had stepped forward to just shoot down either Will or Eddie and take the map for themselves. Clint wasn't the type of man to do such a thing himself, but he knew damn well that there were plenty of others out there who would.

Much more blood had been spilled over much less money, that was for sure. Clint had seen it happen too many times. Now that he knew that the whole mess was over a *piece* of a map, it all started to make a lot more sense.

Why gun down someone for something that won't even lead you directly to what you want? And who was to say if the other half was even out there? For all Clint knew, that map could be waiting to be completed for years or decades. There were two such tall tales for every miner that sat and talked in a saloon. Even they didn't take them seriously anymore.

On the other hand, judging by the scene Clint had found upon his arrival in Richwater, at least two men were taking this tale pretty seriously indeed.

Now that he had his information, Clint decided to let it settle in his brain for a bit. Give it some time, he knew, and he would come up with a good plan. Just then, he was definitely leaning more toward the plan of letting Will and Eddie hash it out among themselves. Now that they'd both drawn blood, they probably would go back to harsh language for a while. After that, the sheriff could deal with them.

Walking along the crooked boards as the sun was starting to drop below the horizon, Clint thought that conclusion sounded like a pretty good one. He'd been resting up after the day's events and cleaning himself up in preparation for the events yet to come. All the while, his mind had been chewing on what had happened and what it seemed was expected of him.

What struck Clint was the fact that Father Pryde seemed ready to ask for his further assistance no matter what Clint's name might have been. He thought back to the look on the priest's face during the scuffle between

Will and Eddie, and Clint swore he saw something else going on behind those light colored eyes.

Perhaps he'd spent too much time trying to put himself into Eddie's train of thought, but Clint became more and more convinced that there was another player in that fight, apart from Will and Eddie. That suspicion had been gnawing at him when he put Eclipse up in a livery, rented a room and even when he'd visited a barber across the street from his hotel.

Now that it was time for dinner and he was about to walk into the place where he was to meet Josie, Clint was getting awfully sick of that particular itch in his craw. Hopefully, the night would prove to be enough of a distraction to scratch it.

He stepped into the saloon and was immediately bombarded by the sounds of several women singing along with a bouncy tune being played on the piano.

For a moment, Clint wondered if he should step outside to look at the front of the building to make sure he was in the right place. Compared to the way the saloon had looked when he'd had his beers with Father Pryde, Clint could hardly recognize it now that it was full to busting with what had to be about a third of the town's population.

The dancers kicked up their heels on stage, tossing their brightly colored skirts back and forth, all to the appreciative cheers of a mostly male audience. The bar was so crowded that Clint couldn't tell if Sam was still working or not.

Then, he spotted something that made everything else seem to quiet down and stand still. Sitting at a table toward the front of the room, Josie waved to Clint and smiled widely when she saw that he was able to pick her out.

The only itch he felt at that moment was the need to get closer to the sensuous brunette who'd been waiting for him to arrive.

FOURTEEN

They'd tried to sit at the table in the Gold Coast for all of five minutes before Clint asked about moving to somewhere a little more quiet. Josie didn't seem to mind that one bit, and they wound up getting their food delivered to a little room in back used as a sitting area for the dancing girls. Josie knew a few of the girls who were performing that night, so it wasn't too hard for her to get herself and Clint behind the scenes and away from most of the others in the saloon.

Although they could still hear the sounds of voices and piano music, it was a whole lot easier to hear each other now that they had a bit of privacy. Their dinner consisted of stew, baked potatoes and some bread. Simple, yet very delicious. Clint's mouth began to water as soon as it was brought into the room and set upon the little round table Josie had moved between two chairs.

"It seems like you've got some clout around here," Clint said.

Josie shrugged and lifted a spoonful of stew to her mouth. "Not really," she said before blowing gently on the smoking stew. "I wanted to work here and didn't get the job. A few of my friends were hired, though, so it shouldn't be long before they get me another chance to audition."

"You're a dancer?"

"I sure am. How about yourself? What do you do when you're not pulling grown men apart from each other as they try to tear each other's throat out?"

"Actually, you'd be surprised how much time I spend in the middle of things like that."

"Maybe," Josie said with a sweet smile. "Maybe not. I've heard that you're quite a gunman." Seeing the expression on Clint's face, she immediately tried to put his mind at ease. "Sorry, but this is a small town and word gets around. Don't feel too bad, though. I've had plenty of rumors passed around about me or my friends."

"Nothing too bad, I hope?"

"Nothing I can't handle. The best thing to do is just not give a damn about what folks say. That frees you up to do whatever you want."

When she said that, Clint could tell that Josie was staring at him intently. Her soft, dark eyes were framed by long, luscious lashes, and her lips seemed especially red and sensual when she spoke. It didn't matter what she said. The motion of forming the words stirred something deep inside of Clint which made him very aware that they were alone in the room.

They ate for a few minutes without saying much. Instead, they used the time to enjoy their food and listen to the music which filtered in from the main room. Without having to contend with the crowds and hectic activity out front, it seemed as though the music was a kind of serenade. Perhaps a bit louder than most serenades, but still entertaining.

Clint noticed the instant Josie started to say something because he found her cherry-red lips to be almost distractingly beautiful. She spoke a little quieter than before, and at that moment the girls on stage all raised their voices for a lively number.

"Sorry," Clint said. "I couldn't hear you."

Lowering her head a bit, Josie took hold of her chair and scooted it closer to Clint's side. From there, she leaned over and spoke softly into his ear. Her breath was warm and her hair smelled like fresh, winter air.

"I said I had a confession to make, Clint."

Her voice had not only become somewhat softer, but there was a sexy breathiness to it that hadn't been there before. Just hearing it made Clint want to run his hands on her body and feel her skin pressed against his lips.

"Go ahead," he said, doing his best to cover up what he was truly feeling at that moment.

"I saw you step in between Will and Eddie. I saw the way you moved, the way you didn't show the first bit of fear even though those men had guns and were mad as hell. Nobody else was going to go near them two, and Father Pryde only did it because he was caught talking to Will when Eddie found them."

"Really? He was there with Will to begin with?"

She nodded slowly as her eyes moved from Clint's eyes down over his face and then back again. Her breaths were getting faster, and her breasts were brushing against Clint's arm when she inhaled. "I was across the street when it happened. I saw how it started, and Father Pryde was about to run before he saw it was too late.

"None of the others around there were going to do a thing. Not even a man who acts as a deputy while the sheriff's away."

The surprised look was so plain on Clint's face that Josie giggled a bit when she saw it.

"There are deputies?" he asked.

She nodded. "And they were scared. You weren't. I've never seen anything like that before. It was so exciting. It made my blood get hot in my veins just watching it."

"So is that your confession?" Clint asked as he turned and positioned himself so that he was facing her, with one leg in between hers.

When she shook her head, she moved slowly and kept her eyes locked on his. "My confession is that I went here to find you afterward and that I also had this room set aside so that we could be alone."

Clint moved in close enough to kiss her, but fought back the impulse to follow through just yet. "Did you really go to all that trouble?"

She nodded, but their faces were so close that her lips touched Clint's for a moment as she moved. "Yes, I did."

"And are we really going to be alone in here?"

"For a little while, anyway. At least until the show's over."

"Then we'd better not waste any more time."

With that, Clint gave in to what he'd been craving ever since he'd first seen Josie earlier that day. He kissed her fully on the lips and felt her respond to him immediately. At first, she just kissed him back, but soon she let her own desires come out as well and her tongue slipped into Clint's mouth.

The music played on, but Clint and Josie were too busy to notice.

FIFTEEN

It was one of those kisses that just never seemed to stop. The moment both of them gave in to the moment, Clint and Josie were wrapped up completely in each other's embrace. All Clint could taste was the sweet flavor of her lips, and the smell of her skin wrapped around him like smoke. She kept her hands moving back and forth across his shoulders, massaging his muscles and tracing the occasional line down the back of Clint's neck.

Before he knew what was happening, Clint felt her weight come down on top of him as Josie got out of her chair and sat straddling him on his. Her skirts bunched up around her waist as her strong legs closed tightly around him.

Josie took a moment to settle, moving slightly until she felt the bulge of his hardening penis rubbing between her legs. Smiling and leaning back, she placed her hands on Clint's shoulders and rubbed herself against his growing erection.

"I feel like I've been wanting this for so long," she said. "But it's only been hours."

"Too long," Clint said as his hands slipped up under her skirts so he could feel her smooth, bare skin.

Josie let out a hungry breath and her eyes widened when she felt Clint's fingers move along the inside of her thighs and up even farther. "Much too long to wait."

Tracing a line with his fingers along the edge of her panties, Clint reached beneath the flimsy material. Watching Josie's smile widen with satisfaction as he rubbed the moist lips of her vagina, Clint said, "Then let's not wait a moment longer."

That was all Josie needed to hear before she reached down to pull open Clint's jeans and shift her weight so that she could take hold of his cock. As soon as she had her fingers around his hard penis, she stroked it up and down while using her other hand to pull his jeans down farther.

Clint lifted himself up off the chair just long enough for her to get his pants down and when he sat down again, he kicked them the rest of the way off. Josie's head was hanging down over his face and she was kissing his neck in between nibbling on his lips. He could feel her hand still stroking his cock as the rest of her body squirmed on top of him.

Finally, Josie positioned him so that she could lower herself down onto him and impale herself on his rigid penis. She dropped all the way down, slowly taking him inside of her and savoring every last moment. When he was buried deeply between her legs, she opened her eyes and kissed him passionately on the lips.

Clint's hands were busy moving beneath her skirts, feeling the solid muscles that tensed beneath Josie's flesh. Her skin was soft and yielding to his touch and her buttocks felt perfectly rounded as he cupped them in his palms.

All Clint had to do was lift her up slightly and then Josie began rocking back and forth on his lap. She managed to get her feet braced on the chair, which allowed her to lift up slightly without breaking the smooth motion of her hips grinding against his.

Clint leaned back in the chair, letting the sensation of being inside of her wash through him. Offhandedly, he noticed that the music was dying down a bit, but the dancers were still singing loud enough to be heard. His attention was pulled away from that when he saw Josie straighten up and use both hands to pull the ribbon holding the front of her blouse closed.

When the thin strip of silky material was loosened, her blouse fell open to reveal the soft, sensual contours of her breasts. Like many other things women tended to wear, Josie's blouse had been secured tightly about her bosom to hold her firmly in place. Now that the garment was allowed to open, Clint could see that her breasts were even larger than he'd imagined and he could just make out the edges of her small, dark nipples through the loose halves of material.

Clint moved his hands flat along her sides, slowly working his way along her hips, then up to her ribs, until he felt the bottom curve of her breasts on his thumb and forefinger. Staying there no matter how much he wanted to feel the hardness of her erect nipples was enough to drive them both to new levels.

Rocking faster on top of him now, Josie placed her hands on top of his and moved them up until she felt him holding her breasts. She leaned her head back and arched her spine while squeezing her pussy tightly around him.

After taking hold of her hips once again, Clint lifted her up as he pulled himself onto his feet and off his chair. Josie's grip tightened around him and she looked at him with surprise mixed with excitement as she was lifted up with him.

They didn't go far. All Clint did was take a half-step forward and set her down upon the edge of the table. Josie took over from there and leaned back, while sweeping the plates and silverware onto the floor with one arm. Lying with her back on the newly cleared table, she threaded her fingers through her hair and spread her legs open wider so Clint could move in between them.

He took a moment to drink in the sight of her in front of him. Her dress was a mess and gathered up around her waist. Her top was open so widely that it had almost been ripped. Even so, he barely noticed any of that. Instead, Clint was focusing more on the strong, shapely legs emerging from those skirts and wrapping around him. He was much more interested in the firm, rounded breasts topped with their small erect nipples. Finally, he slid his hands up along her thighs and massaged the warm, tender flesh.

Josie was so anxious for him to be inside of her again that she squirmed impatiently on the table, pushing her hips forward and pouting with her bottom lip. She didn't have to say a word, however, before Clint moved his hips forward and guided the tip of his cock between her smooth, moist folds.

They both let out stifled groans as he slid all the way inside of her. She was so wet that he glided in effortlessly, the warmth of her delicate skin wrapping around and caressing him. Clint lowered himself down just enough so he could meet her lips as Josie propped herself up onto one elbow.

Her tongue darted out to taste his mouth as he pumped between her legs. She had one foot set up on the table so she could thrust her hips along to his rhythm, and soon they were thrusting harder and harder while staring into each other's eyes.

It was at that moment that Clint noticed something that he'd promised he wouldn't forget about. It was something simple that he knew he needed to keep track of from the moment he first felt Josie's lips against his own.

It was the music.

The music had stopped.

All that Clint could hear was the smattering of applause and the rumble of footsteps on the stage. What was worse was the fact that those footsteps were getting closer.

Judging by the look on her face, Josie had noticed the same things as well, but when Clint started to pull away, she reached out and took hold of his wrist. "They'll be playing up to the crowd for another minute or two," she said breathlessly. "Just please don't stop. Not now."

Clint shook his head to protest, but felt Josie's hips pumping back and forth, sliding him in and out of her in short, little thrusts. Feeling his body responding to the sensation of what she was doing to him, Clint shook his head even as he grabbed hold of her hips and pounded into her.

As they listened for the slightest change in the sounds coming from just on the other side of the wall, every one of Clint's and Josie's senses was lifted to new heights. Not only did they pay closer attention to their surroundings, but they were feeling each other even more intensely as well.

As he slid in and out of her, Clint could feel her hot, wet embrace running along every inch of his shaft.

Josie arched her back and grabbed onto the side of the table as the pleasure she'd been feeling started to boil over inside of her. It was as though every place he was touching her was tingling with anticipation. When she felt him bury himself all the way inside of her, a powerful orgasm was unleashed which swept all the way up to make her eyes roll back and then headed down to the tips of her toes.

The applause was just starting to fade when Clint's grip tightened around Josie's rounded hips. Although he could hear some of the dancers' voices getting closer, he was too close himself to stop his urgent thrusting. Clint's brain was screaming for him to stop before a dozen dancers came by to find them both in the open, which made his own climax explode like a clap of thunder behind his eyes.

Clint gritted his teeth against the moan that wanted to explode from the back of his throat, and when it passed, he saw Josie spread out in front of him as though she didn't have enough energy to move.

Not only were the footsteps closer now, but there was a sudden surge of noise as the dancers began running backstage.

SIXTEEN

The dancers flooded backstage like a stampede of shapely legs wrapped in flowing skirts. Their voices blended into an excited mishmash of nonsensical syllables as each one talked to another about the performance they'd just given and some of the reactions they'd gotten from the crowd.

As the stampede rounded that corner, they all saw the table and chairs along with the two people who'd dined at them. Clint was sitting in his chair with a napkin over his lap and Josie was standing next to the table, nervously straightening the front of her dress. Although plenty of the dancers gave them funny looks, most of them continued along their way and didn't stop until they got to the nearby dressing rooms.

Only one of those dancers was paying extra attention to what she would see when she turned the next corner, since she'd been the one to set up the table for her friend Josie Moynahan. Josie's friend let the rest go on and she stood there casting suspicious glances at the guilty looking couple. Once the other dancers were all gone, the one who'd stayed behind walked right up to Josie and began tapping her foot.

"Well, don't you look like the cat that swallowed the canary," the dancer said.

Josie quickly pushed a few strands of wayward hair aside and put on an innocent, although unconvincing, smile. "What do you mean?" she asked, pretending not to notice the broken dishes on the floor or the fact that both she and Clint looked as though they'd been in a windstorm.

"At least tell me the dinner was worth all the trouble I went through."

Josie's smile shifted from innocent to devilish in a heartbeat when she said, "Oh, it was worth it."

That was all that needed to be said for the moment, and the dancer shook her head while helping Josie locate a few hooks and buttons that she hadn't fastened yet. "Aren't you going to introduce me to your friend?"

Now that she knew the other dancer was up to speed, Josie looked a little embarrassed. "Clint Adams, this is Maggie Jeffries. She helped me arrange this little surprise for you."

"Thanks for the dinner," Clint said, shaking her hand without getting up from his chair. "You'll have to let me return the favor for you before I leave. Maybe all three of us could get a steak. My treat, of course."

"Sure," Maggie said while obviously trying hard not to laugh at the two of them. "That sounds great. But would you mind if we had our steaks somewhere in the open?"

Now Clint was certain of two things. Not only did Maggie have a real good idea of what had been going on right before she got there, but she was probably going to have all the other details filled in for her once she got a chance to talk to Josie on her own. That much was made abundantly clear by the gleam in Maggie's eye as well as the sly grin on her face.

"No problem," Clint said. "Just name the time and place. I'll be there."

"Sounds good," Maggie answered, finally letting them off the hook. "I think I'll be going now so I can change out of these sweaty clothes." She leaned in closer to Josie, but spoke just loud enough for Clint to hear as well. "You might want to do the same, sweetie."

Josie's answer to that was a light, swatting backhand which caught the dancer on her exposed shoulder. "I'll talk to you later."

"You know it. Nice to meet you, Mr. Adams." Waving to them both, Maggie headed toward a narrow hall which led to the nearby dressing rooms.

Once she was gone, Clint laughed and said, "I feel like I'm going to be in trouble here."

"Oh, don't fret about it, that was just Maggie having some fun with you. We'd better get out of here, though, or we might just get in trouble. I don't think the owner would appreciate us making a mess back here without paying extra for the privilege."

Clint stood up and took the napkin from his lap, which had been placed there to cover the fact that he hadn't had enough time to fasten his pants or belt all the way before the dancers came storming in. After buckling and buttoning himself up, Clint tossed the napkin onto the table and wrapped his arms around Josie's waist.

"You want to continue this back at my hotel?" he asked.

Her eyes widened and she smiled broadly. "You tucker me out this much and you're not finished?"

"Nope."

"You really are a legend, Clint Adams." She kissed him warmly and said, "But legend or not, you're helping me clean this up."

SEVENTEEN

Will Ambrose had been sitting in his rented room all night. As much as he wanted to go out for a warm meal or maybe catch the show at the Gold Coast, he knew he would regret it dearly if he was gone when the visitor he'd been expecting finally arrived.

Not to say that there weren't plenty of people stopping by to see him already. One of the young men who called themselves deputies—just so long as it got them a free drink—came over to warn Will against picking any more fights. Will told the kid to save the warning for who really needed it and sent the kid over to Eddie's house.

The owner of the boardinghouse came by to collect her rent, and of course Father Pryde had stopped over to give another sermon just in case Will had forgotten about the last dozen or so he'd gotten already. Every one of those folks had been dealt with and sent on their way as quickly as Will could manage. And every time someone had knocked on that door, Will had been expecting the worst.

Looking out the window, Will could feel the night's cold seeping through the glass as he stared off into the cloudless, inky black sky. He was almost afraid to look down onto the street one floor below him, simply because he might just find what he'd be looking for. As much as he'd started to hope that that one visitor had forgotten about him, he knew that might be too much to ask.

As if responding to the thoughts running through Will's head, his door rattled with a strong knocking that seemed to jar the brain inside Will's skull. He waited for a moment in silence, looking at the reflection of the door on the window rather than at the door itself.

But the knocking didn't stop. It paused for a moment, but quickly came again, rattling the door against its hinges with renewed vigor.

Will took a deep breath, turned around and went to the door. He could almost feel the presence of the man on the other side, like it was a wave of heat emanating through the wood. He grabbed the handle, let out his breath, and opened the door.

The man standing in the hall looked like a shadow that had pulled itself free and started walking around on its own. A black coat was buttoned up to his neck, and the only piece of his face that could be seen from beneath the black, wide-brimmed hat was a pointed chin and the lower half of a grim smile.

"Hello, Will," Kyle Hammund said. "If I didn't know better, I might think you weren't happy to see me."

Will began to force a smile on his face, but quit when he realized he wouldn't be able to pull it off without twitching. Instead, he averted his eyes and opened the door a little more so the man in black could walk past him. "I just thought you'd be here earlier is all. Come on inside."

Nodding, Kyle took his time and stepped past Will into the little rented room. He pointed to a box sitting in the hall and said, "Bring that in here. I carried it far enough already."

Knowing better than to voice what he thought of that order, Will just did as he was told and picked up the box that Kyle had left outside his door. The crate was heavy and awkward since most of its weight was from a pick and shovel that were about to fall out at any second. Will moved the crate just far enough so that the door could close, then dropped it next to his bed.

Kyle was already standing at the window, in the same spot where Will had been only moments ago. His arms were crossed over his chest, and with mild amusement he watched Will struggle with the box. "You been keeping out of trouble?" Kyle asked.

Shrugging, Will replied, "Yeah, I guess."

All Kyle had to do was tilt his head slightly for Will to give his answer a little more thought.

"There was a bit of a scuffle this morning," Will added. "But it didn't amount to much. Just some bumps and bruises."

"That's not what I hear."

"Huh?"

"All I had to do was keep my ears open and I hear that you and some other asshole nearly killed each other."

"It's not as bad as all that. You know how word gets spread in a town like this."

"Yeah," Kyle said with a scowl. When he uncrossed his arms, Kyle unbuttoned his coat and let it fall open to reveal the glint of gold at his side. "And I also know that every little rumor has some grain of truth in it somewhere. You were supposed to keep quiet until I got here."

"Eddie was getting too close, and if it wasn't for Father Pryde, I might not have known about it at all until I had a bullet in my back."

"You told a priest about this? Now's not exactly the best time for confession, Will."

"It wasn't like that. Everyone here knows about the map, but they just don't really believe it." Immediately spotting the darkness that had begun to creep over Kyle's face, Will quickly said, "This is a mining town. Hell, there are stories about maps like this one that have been around since Richwater wasn't even here. Every tin panner here's gotten hold of a map that turned out to be a pipe dream."

That seemed to cool the fire that had been burning in Kyle's eyes, but not by much. "Then how come this priest takes such an interest? What did you tell him?"

"I didn't tell him anything. He came to me."

Those last couple words hung in the air for a few moments as Kyle's eyes slowly narrowed into intense slits. Finally, Hammund asked, "Why did he come to you?"

"He said he knew that there was going to be some trouble headed my way and that Eddie might want to gun me down to get ahold of my part of the map."

"If everyone knows about the damn thing, doesn't anyone know that you only have a piece of it?"

"Sure, but I think they figure that when the other piece is delivered, the man holding it won't really care who has the other half, just so long as he gets to the gold."

Kyle didn't even try to deny that that was the case.

EIGHTEEN

Kyle held his hand out and said, "Give me the piece of the map that you've got."

"Oh hell no," Will said. "I'm not stupid. We head out to fetch the gold together or we won't go at all. I'll eat the damn thing before I just hand it over."

"All right then. I'll come back for you in a day or two."

Having kept his ground on one point, Will put a little more force into his voice when he started to argue for another one. "A day or two?" he asked, looking Kyle straight in the eye. "Why can't we go sooner than that? Why not go now?"

Kyle returned Will's stare and added even more fire, until the shorter man backed down. He pressed his advantage until Will had actually taken a step back and nearly tripped over the chair that was behind him.

"Things in this town are going to heat up," Kyle said. "I can feel it. In fact, I might have added a little fuel to the fire myself."

Averting his eyes from the man in black, Will found himself staring down at the box he'd dragged in from the hall. It was then that he noticed the stain on one side that looked like a fresh spatter of dark red paint. That sight, along with what Kyle had just said, sent a shiver down Will's spine.

"Is that blood?" Will asked timidly.

Kyle glanced down at the spot that had captured Will's attention and slowly brought his eyes back up to look at the other man. "Actually, that's something else I was meaning to talk to you about."

The only thing Will could see was a sudden movement before his field of vision was nearly completely black. Kyle had leapt forward so quickly that Will didn't have the chance to do anything until the other man was practically on top of him.

Kyle's hand locked around Will's neck and pulled upward until Will was forced to either look up or get the breath squeezed out of him. Glaring into Will's eyes, Kyle tightened his grip until he could smell the fear seeping out of the other man's pores like cold sweat.

"I had a little problem when I went to pick up those supplies," Kyle said in a voice that was chillingly calm. "It seemed like the store owner invited a welcoming committee to gun me down before I could even pay for my order."

Will shook his head as much as he could and tried to get a few words out from between his sputtering lips. But Kyle wouldn't have any of it, and he lifted his hand up a little more, until Will was standing on his tiptoes just to keep some air flowing.

"Don't try and talk," Kyle instructed as he let up a bit on his grip. "You'll probably just say something to make me lose my patience with you."

That caused Will to nod slowly and suck in a few breaths once his throat was open enough to do so.

"Matt had a few hired guns at his store waiting for me. Now, since he didn't know exactly when I was going to show up, it could have just been a coincidence that those boys were there at that time. But I'm not a big believer in coincidence, so that means that someone else told Matt when I was coming."

Although he kept his grip loose enough for Will to breathe, Kyle dug his fingertips into the sides of Will's neck just to bring the other man some pain. As he dug in his fingers, Kyle clenched his teeth together into a feral snarl.

"It's a short list of folks who knew I was coming today, and you're at the top of it, Will." Suddenly, Kyle's free hand was moving, and in a heartbeat, he'd drawn his pistol and driven its barrel deep into Will's stomach. "Now, I'm going to take my hand away. When I do, you'd better start telling me a good explanation for that ambush or I'll blow your dinner out your back and onto that window."

Even when he felt the hand move away from his throat, Will was held in place by the intensity of the eyes that were still locked onto him. Lies went through his head like a flood, but not one of them was good enough for Will to gamble with his life. He had no doubt that these moments could be his last, whether or not he did exactly what Kyle wanted.

It was the most acute fear a man could know, and it settled into Will's body like cold rain that had soaked through his shirt.

"I told Matt you'd be coming," Will finally said. "But I didn't know he would try to kill you. I swear to Jesus I didn't know about that."

Will watched Kyle's face, searching for any trace of an emotion. He didn't find a damn thing, but he did feel the gun barrel jab into his gut a little more before it was suddenly taken away.

"All right," Kyle said as he holstered the .45. "I believe you."

With that, Kyle turned and headed for the door. "There should be a list in that box," he said before stepping out into the hall. "Make sure everything's in there before we leave. I'll come and get you in twenty-four hours at the Gold Coast. Do yourself a favor and don't talk to anyone else."

Kyle left the shabby room and strode toward the stairs. There was still plenty that needed to be done. Mostly, Kyle needed to track down the other person who he was certain had listened to plenty of Will's babbling. And while he was at it, he just might do some confessing of his own.

NINETEEN

Clint started the next day in the warmth of the sunlight that poured through his window and spilled over his bed. There was also the warmth of the soft body laying next to him, which stirred slightly when he began to shift his weight and crawl out of bed. Josie had one arm draped across his chest and reflexively held on to him tighter before he could get out from under the covers.

Looking over at her, Clint took a moment to study the way the light soaked into her dark hair and gave her skin a warm glow. As if feeling his eyes on her, Josie rolled onto her back and reached up to thread both hands through her hair.

"You trying to get away from me?" she asked, her voice heavy with sleep.

Clint smiled and swung both feet over the mattress so he could set them onto the floor. "Not at all. You're welcome to stay here if you like."

"I have a home in town, you know," she answered sarcastically. "And it just so happens that it's nicer than this room you rented."

"And it's especially kind of you to point that out after I already paid for this room. Should I be offended that you don't want to invite me into your home?"

"What?" Josie said, sitting up and leaning forward so she could see Clint's face. When she got a look at the sly grin that he was wearing, she slapped him on the shoulder and then wrapped her arms around him. Pressing herself against Clint's back, she rested her chin on his shoulder and said, "I thought you meant what you said."

"Nah. It takes a hell of a lot more than that to offend me. Besides, I would have hated to put your home through what this room went through the other night."

Smiling widely herself, Josie lifted her head up and looked around. The sheets were laying crookedly on the bed after having been pulled out on every side. Clothes were scattered from one side of the room to another, and anything that had been on the end tables or dresser was now on the floor.

Clint looked around as well, surveying the damage while reliving the pleasant memory of how that damage had been done. When they'd gotten back to the room after coming from the Gold Coast, Clint and Josie had continued their spontaneous lovemaking without a care as to where they were or what was in their way.

Their hands hadn't left each other's body since the moment their door closed, and since the dresser was the first thing in their path, that was where Clint had set Josie as he let his tongue wander over her breasts and between her legs. She'd hooked her legs over his shoulders and pressed her head against the wall as he pumped into her for the next several minutes.

Clint's eyes lingered on that dresser as he relived the experience in his head. Even though it had only happened the night before, it felt like a dream. It seemed like one hell of a good dream, but a dream nonetheless.

"That end table looks like it might fall apart," Josie said as she traced her fingernail over Clint's bare back.

Her eyes were aimed at the small round table next to

the bed. She could still feel the polished wood against her palms as she'd pressed her hands down on that table for support as Clint settled in behind her. Josie had gripped the edges of the table with all her strength and pushed it against the wall when she'd arched her back and felt Clint's hands on her hips and his rigid penis entering her moist vagina.

"Did we really do all that?" she asked with a naughty laugh. "Or did I just dream it?"

"Funny. I was just thinking that same thing."

Tightening her arms around Clint's shoulders, Josie pulled him back down onto the bed and straddled his chest. "I guess there's one way we can tell for sure," she said while moving her hands over her breasts. "Start over from the beginning, and if it feels just as good, we'll know it wasn't a dream."

Clint let his hands roam over her calves and then up along the smooth, familiar curve of her buttocks. He could hear her pull in a deep, satisfied breath the moment he put his hands on her and could feel his own body responding to it as well.

"I hope you didn't have much planned for today," she whispered. "Because I've got enough plans to keep us busy all day long."

"Actually, there was some things I had to do. There's a favor I promised to do for Father Pryde which I was supposed to do yesterday."

"If you think you'll change my mind by bringing up a priest's name, you'll have to try harder than that."

"Well, I was hoping to change my own mind," Clint said. "I really do need to do this favor for him. It could be bad if I put it off too long."

"But you'd rather stay here with me, right?" Before Clint could answer that question, Josie reached behind her to feel between Clint's legs. She smiled and wrapped her fingers around his stiff cock, rubbing it up and down. "I can tell you'd much rather stay here with me."

"You'd rather have me break my word to a man of the cloth just so we can spend some more time fooling around in here?"

Josie's eyes opened and she looked down at Clint. The movement caused her hair to spill down over her shoulders, the ends dangling in front of her little, erect nipples. "That's funny talk coming from a man who had to get me out of my clothes so fast that I still haven't found all the buttons. If you want to make Father Pryde happy, why don't you tell him how you spent your night having wholesome dinner conversation with me, an unmarried woman?"

"You've got a point there," Clint admitted with a laugh. "But I've still got some work to—"

The rest of his sentence was forgotten the moment Josie moved herself back and fitted his cock between her thighs. Keeping her back straight and her hands on Clint's stomach, she began to ride him in a slow rocking motion.

"All right," Clint sighed. "You talked me into it."

TWENTY

Clint didn't get as early a start as he'd wanted, but he did manage to get out of his room for a late breakfast. He and Josie had a pleasant meal in the dining room of his hotel, which wasn't much bigger than the dining room of a normal-sized home. Because they'd been late in coming down, however, they both managed to get seated and served without much fuss.

Conversation was casual, and most of it was Josie telling him about some of the local gossip. Apparently, Eddie's map was pretty much common knowledge after all, but it was just one of several dozen such tales circulating, as they did around any mining camp. The few locals who took it seriously weren't about to kill for it.

The few locals, of course, except for Eddie and Will themselves.

Those two were most definitely ready to kill each other. Clint had been there and seen it for himself. But as he listened to Josie talk, he got the impression that nobody else in town thought those two would have laid a finger on each other if tensions hadn't boiled over that one time. Clint blamed his own luck in stumbling upon the situation when it got to its worst point, and Josie laughed it off with a shrug.

"I'm glad you came here no matter when it was," she said warmly. "And I'm sure Father Pryde is glad as well."

"Really?" Clint asked, as something in the back of his head took special notice. "Why do you say that?"

For a moment, Josie looked as though she wasn't sure what she'd said to warrant the question. Then she shrugged again and replied, "I heard that he asked you to step in and take the sheriff's place while he's away. He's asked a few others to do that, but most of his choices weren't too good."

"They weren't, huh?"

"Not really. He asked a few of the old-timers who could barely lift their tallywackers, not to mention their guns. Then he asked one of the deputies, but that one was too young and scared to want to fill the sheriff's boots."

"That's interesting," Clint said as the warning chill in the back of his head started working its way up into something bigger.

Josie didn't pick up at all on what was going through Clint's mind. Instead, she was focused on finishing up the biscuits she'd ordered. "Actually, it's not really interesting at all, but that's sweet of you to listen. None of us thinks any less of the father for trying, though. He didn't know any better, since he's so new in town and all."

"That reminds me. When I was talking to Father Pryde yesterday, he said something about being here for a lot longer than a month or so."

Josie chuckled and then looked around to see if anyone had heard her. Since the only other people in the vicinity were the hotel owners, and they were talking among themselves at a table closer to the lobby, she lowered her voice and continued. "It's not polite to say unkind things about a preacher and all, but if you ask me that one's not all there sometimes."

"Go ahead and spill it," Clint prodded good-naturedly. "It's too late to turn back now."

"Well, it's just that he'll go on and on about something that happened in some other parish, but when someone else asks him about it, he can barely remember it. He just gets this look on his face like his brains leaked out his ears." Josie demonstrated with just enough exaggeration to make Clint laugh.

"He's a good man, though," she added. "His sermons are truly inspiring and the Sunday services are always full."

"From what I heard, it's Miss Marple's pies that keep people coming back for more."

Josie's smile faded a bit and her face twisted as though she'd just eaten some sour fruit. "That's what she'd like to think, but she's so full of herself that she thinks an awful lot that makes her look better than she is."

"Am I sensing some hard feelings between you and the father's favorite baker?"

"Just wait until you meet her," Josie said with a scowl. "You'll see what I mean. Then again, you might not have to put yourself through that. Will you be staying another night here in town?"

"I guess so. That is, unless something happens or I get run out on a rail for some reason."

Reaching over to rub Clint's arm, Josie smiled and said, "Well, first of all, Richwater doesn't have any rails. But also, I'd like it if you stayed until tomorrow. That way we'd get another night together."

"With incentive like that, how could I resist?"

Clint finished the meal and thought about the bits of information he'd gotten from Josie. Unfortunately, some of it didn't settle with him as well as the biscuits and coffee.

TWENTY-ONE

Clint was glad he'd taken some extra time before going out to meet up with the remaining two participants in yesterday's scuffle. Apart from the fact that he'd gotten some good time with Josie before even leaving the room, Clint knew it was a good idea to let everyone settle down a bit before asking too many questions.

Now that Will and Father Pryde had had a chance to unwind and let their pulses slow a bit, Clint figured he might have an easier time in approaching them. Apart from all of that, it also bought some more time before the sheriff was due to arrive. Clint wasn't familiar with the area's lawman or how long it took him to go from one town to another, but it couldn't be too much longer before the sheriff returned.

That is, of course, assuming that the sheriff hadn't run into any unforeseen trouble of his own.

Trying not to dwell too much on the negative, Clint focused his attention on what he was doing at the moment. It was a pleasant day with the sun beaming through a thin layer of clouds which crawled across the sky. It was just cool enough to chill the skin, but not so much so that Clint wanted to get out of the breeze altogether.

The town was bustling around him as he walked down the street, and all the activity made Richwater seem like it was bigger than he'd previously thought. That notion left Clint's mind the moment he turned a corner and moved away from the town's business district. Once the stores and saloons were mostly behind him, Clint had to search to find a single person nearby.

He hadn't gone more than a few yards before the boards beneath his feet gave way to packed dirt. The only way to know where the street flowed was by following the ruts that had been worn in the ground between the squat buildings. Following the directions that Pryde had given the day before, Clint found himself in an area that was mostly small homes and even smaller storage sheds.

The next corner took him into a slightly more populated area which also saw the return of the boards lining either side of the street. Those boards looked more like driftwood, however, and had probably been laid down after a few other larger buildings had been torn down. It wasn't hard to spot the small offices next to the boardinghouse where Clint had been told that Will was living.

Although more than a little run-down, the boardinghouse seemed pleasant enough. Much of that could have been attributed to the enticing smell of cooking coming from behind the front door. Clint opened the door and stepped inside, immediately spotting a gray-haired woman walking toward him while brushing flour off both hands.

"Yes? Hello?" she said in a gruff tone. "Are you here to rent a room, because I don't think there's any open just now."

"I don't need a room, but I might just have to come back for dinner," Clint said. "Whatever you're cooking, it smells great."

The woman looked to be somewhere in her late sixties. She was a full head shorter than Clint, but carried herself as though she could lift him up out of his boots. Her hands were thick and calloused, twisting a dirty apron tied around her wide waist. Her dress was a simple yellow garment that looked as though it had been her Sunday best many, many Sundays ago.

Her eyes regarded Clint carefully, although there was a definite softening in her mannerisms once she heard the compliment he'd given so earnestly. "Dinner's served at five," she said without so much of an edge to her voice. "Come back then and I guarantee you won't leave hungry."

"You can save me a seat. Until then, there was another reason for me being here."

"I knew it. Like I said, there's no rooms left, but there's a fine hotel just up the bl—"

"I've got a room," Clint interrupted. "I need to visit with one of your guests."

"Yeah? Which one?"

By the way she was looking at him, it seemed as though the woman already had a good guess as to what Clint was going to say. He didn't have to get out more than one syllable before all of her initial gruffness had returned.

"Will Ambr—"

"Oh no," she cut in. "You just leave poor Will alone. He's had enough trouble for a good long while."

"I don't mean to cause any trouble. Actually, I was the one who stepped in on his behalf the other day."

"Is that so? I heard about that. Will told me he damn near caught a bullet in the back from that thief Eddie Vale. It sounded like a nightmare. Truly horrible."

Considering the locals' penchant for spreading rumors and telling tales, Clint had no doubt in his mind that the story Will gave the woman made it seem like he'd gone through the fires of hell and back. Rather than let on as to what he really thought about what had happened, Clint went along with the woman's take on it.

"It was terrible, ma'am," he said with a solemn nod.

"That's why I chose to lend a hand. Father Pryde himself requested that I come to talk to Will just to make sure he's not in any more danger."

That turned the woman around completely. She'd already stopped wringing her hands nervously and had reached out to pat Clint's arm. "I'm sorry if I was rude just now. Of course you can go right up and see him."

"No problem, ma'am. A simple misunderstanding. Could have happened to anyone."

But that didn't seem to be enough for the older woman, who clearly felt just as bad as she looked. "Tell you what. Come back later and dinner's free of charge."

"That's awfully kind of you, but it's really not—"

"It's just that after that other one came in last night, I've been a bit on the nervous side."

"Other one?" Clint asked. "What other one?"

"The man who got here late last night and demanded to speak to Will. I tried to get him to wait while I went up to make sure Will was decent, but that one wouldn't have any of it. He just barged right past me carrying some big crate and nearly knocked me down."

Already, Clint had stepped over to the bottom of the staircase, which was at the back of the front room. He glanced up the stairs, looking to see if there was any sign of movement coming from the upper floor. Not only couldn't Clint see anything, but he couldn't hear anything either.

"What did this man look like?" Clint asked, trying to keep his voice and face from showing the tension that was building inside of him.

"Oh, he was tall and probably close to your build. It was hard to see much, though, since his coat was buttoned and he had a hat pulled down over most of his face. I didn't like the looks of him from what I could see, I can tell you that much."

"What was in the crate?"

"All I could see was a shovel or two. Whatever it was, it was heavy."

"And what happened once he went upstairs?"

She started to answer, but suddenly closed her mouth and looked up at Clint with guilty eyes. "I don't pry on my guests, you understand."

"Of course."

"But it sounded like there were some nasty words getting thrown about. That's why I wasn't too happy to see another stranger walk through my door. I hope you get this mess with poor Will straightened out."

"I'll try, ma'am," Clint said as he headed up the stairs. His right hand dropped to his side so he could feel the Colt against his wrist. "Do me a favor and stay down here."

TWENTY-TWO

Clint worked his way up to the second floor, making sure to step on the edges of the stairs so that he wouldn't make too many squeaks along the way. If someone had been paying close enough attention, they wouldn't have had any trouble hearing the conversation between him and the gray-haired woman wearing the apron. That woman's voice had been loud enough to attract attention from the street.

If there was someone upstairs with bad intentions on his mind, he would know that Clint was there. But that didn't mean Clint was going to announce every one of his steps now that he intended on going up to Will's room. Clint had had enough ambushes for the time being and wasn't about to let another happen so easily.

Just over halfway up the stairs, Clint could start to see what was waiting for him on that second floor. From what he could see, it was a straight hallway that ran the entire length of the building, which wasn't enough for more than three or four rooms maximum. His eyes were gazing along the floor and he couldn't see one set of feet standing there. At least, they weren't standing out in the open.

Still heading upward, Clint moved so that he was standing sideways with his back touching the wall. One hand was stretched out to touch the wall as well, and his other was hovering over the holstered Colt. As his heart beat a little quicker in his chest, Clint felt his senses sharpen, as they would right before a fight.

Times like that were when a man's body did everything it could to make sure it survived whatever tense situation was going on. Whoever coined the phrase about being able to hear a pin drop must have been a gunfighter. In those moments before the lead started to fly, the cocking of a hammer sounded like metallic thunder. The slightest twitch of an eye could be seen with perfect precision.

Clint was very much aware of all this as he made it to the top of the stairs and came to a stop. Standing there, he focused his eyes on the hallway stretching out in front of him, waiting for his instincts to tell him it was safe to move on.

He could hear the woman's feet shuffling against the floorboards downstairs. Through the slats beneath his boots he could feel the vibration of someone walking in one of the nearby rooms. And Clint could even see the door to room number two moving ever so slightly on its hinges.

Clint's gun arm relaxed and his fingers opened over the Colt's grip. His back hunched down just a bit for balance if he had to move suddenly.

There was a moment of absolute calm before the door Clint had been watching swung inward and someone came rushing out.

Clint's hand flashed down to grab the Colt and he'd lifted the pistol halfway from its holster when he got a clear look at who was coming out of that room. The first thing he saw was the shape of a man with both arms held up high and in front of him. Next, Clint could see that the man's hands were empty and his eyes were flooded with fear.

"Don't shoot," the man said in a trembling voice. "I don't have much money, but it's all in the room just take it. I won't stop y—"

"Get out of here," Clint said, easing the Colt back into its holster. "Go on."

The man's first couple of steps were tentative, but he picked up steam once he made it to the top of the staircase. From there, he nearly tripped over himself racing down to the front door and quickly out of the building entirely.

Clint didn't take his eyes off the hallway, but listened to follow the other man's progress. Once he heard that one's frantic steps carry him a safe distance away, Clint moved down the hall, keeping his back against the wall.

One quick look into the room was enough to tell him it was now empty. Even through the half-open door, which was still swinging back from the other man's hasty exit, Clint could see the room was practically a closet, with enough room only for a bed and chair. There wasn't enough room to hide another person, so he shut the door and moved on.

Clint's senses were still at their peak, and he could see well enough to discern bits of dust swirling through the air as sunlight poured in through a window at the other end of the hall. He couldn't hear a thing behind the door to room number one, which was enough for him to move past it and beyond.

Pryde had told him that Will lived in room number three of the boardinghouse. Approaching that door cautiously, Clint studied the floor as though he was tracking someone on the open trail. There was no dirt or leaves that could be disturbed, but there was plenty of dusty grit on the wooden slats, which was highlighted by the late morning sun.

Apart from the twin sets of clean rows that would have been made by the boarders walking down the hall, Clint could see a spot directly across from the third door that was fresher than most. It was also the shape of a large square; about the size of a heavy crate.

At least Clint knew that the man in black the woman had seen was in either the third or fourth room. Clint wasn't going to bank on that fact, but the square spot on the floor gave the woman's account a bit more credibility. Since there were only four rooms in all, Clint moved quickly past the last set of doors so he could look down the entire length of the hall.

Leaning against the wall next to the third door, Clint held his breath and listened carefully for a moment. He could definitely hear someone moving inside that room. The steps came through clear as day, and when Clint pressed his ear against the wall, he could tell it was only one person stepping closer to the door.

When the gunshots came, the sound of them exploded through Clint's head in much the same way the bullets exploded through the thin wooden wall. He recoiled from where he'd been standing, taking a step back as one hand went up to press against the side of his aching head.

Clint's other hand moved on its own, dropping down and drawing the Colt in one fluid motion. He struggled to clear the painful roar that was rolling behind his eyes as he stepped back into the rear corner of the hallway.

He would have returned fire, but he couldn't see a target. All he could see were the holes being punched through the wall, working their way closer to where he was standing.

TWENTY-THREE

So far, three shots had been fired. The first went through the door itself. The second punched through the wall next to the frame, and the third whipped through the air and drilled into the door frame of room number four.

Clint was standing with his back to a corner. On one side of him was solid wall and on the other was a large, square window. Dropping down to one knee, Clint lifted the Colt and pointed it toward the third door as a fourth round slapped against the wood a few feet from his face.

Since Clint didn't have a good chance of hitting anything without seeing what to aim at, he knew he had only a fraction of a second to figure the best way to make it through the following couple of seconds. He already knew that one man could only fire six shots before needing to reload or switch to another gun.

But those last two shots had been getting much too close for comfort, even though the man firing was doing so blindly.

That last part stuck in Clint's mind as he glanced back at the last few bullet holes. Although they weren't exactly evenly spaced, they were each at least two feet apart and had been fired as quickly as a man could move his hand and pull a trigger.

All of that blazed through Clint's head in that half a second. He spent the rest of that second stepping to his left, which took him toward the freshest bullet hole. At the last moment, he turned his body so his shoulders were lined up toward the source of the gunfire as the next shot hissed through the hallway.

In Clint's heightened state of mind, he swore he could see the specks parting in the air like a dusty sea as the bullet flew out of one hole in the wall and created another less than three inches from the back of Clint's head.

The sixth shot missed Clint by an even greater distance and shattered the window at the end of the hall. After that, the only sound that could be heard was muffled cursing coming from room number three and the rattle of empty bullet casings being dropped onto the floor.

Clint let out the breath he'd been holding and saw that he was standing directly between two bullet holes. At least one of the last two shots would have hit him where he'd just been standing. But he'd dropped down onto the floor, he wouldn't have been able to rush the door as quickly as he did once he launched himself away from the wall and charged like a rampaging bull.

The door was either open a bit or Clint was just moving too fast to care. He plowed through it as though it had been constructed from paper, and rushed all the way to the back of the room. Once he was there, he turned and slammed his back against the wall, bringing the Colt up to point at the only person he could see.

Will Ambrose stood there with a .44 dangling from where his finger was hooked through the trigger guard. The cylinder was hanging out as well and his other hand was full of fresh ammunition.

"Put your hands up," Clint snarled. "Now!"

The bullets Will had been holding clattered to the floor, the noise of which was soon followed by the heavy thump of the pistol. Will's hands went up and his eyes clenched shut as he prepared himself to meet his maker.

TWENTY-FOUR

Clint's finger tensed on his trigger, pulling it back until he could feel the hammer looming ominously over the back of the shell. That was the only part of him that budged as he stared down the man in front of him until Will was in his place.

Satisfied that Will wasn't about to make any sudden moves, Clint glanced around the rest of the room. As he figured, there wasn't enough room for anyone to hide, which meant that he and Will were the only two occupants.

Once that was settled, Clint allowed himself to relax just enough to straighten up and let some of the fire in his eyes cool off. Will noticed the change immediately and started to let his arms down.

"Not just yet," Clint snapped.

Will flinched and shot both hands so high over his head that they came close to bumping against the ceiling.

Even though he looked like it was taking all his strength to keep on his feet, Will spoke in a surprisingly steady voice. "I didn't know it was you out there."

"Really? That's great. So I could have been the lady who owns this place coming up to clean for all you knew.

Is that supposed to make you look better or something?"

"No," Will answered, taking a moment to think. Suddenly, Clint's words seemed to sink in and he let out a frightened breath. "Jesus, you're right. Was anyone else out there?"

"No. You got lucky on that one. But don't let it go to your head. Just because you missed me doesn't mean I enjoyed getting shot at." Clint could see Will's arms starting to tremble and his eyes nervously darting from one side to another. "Kick that gun toward me and sit down."

Will was only too pleased to do as he was told and even swept the bullets away with the side of his boot for good measure. When he sat down, he kept his hands over his head, which struck Clint as a funny sight even after what had just happened.

"You can put your hands down," Clint said, keeping a straight face. "So how about you explain what the hell all that was about. If you didn't think it was me out there, then who were you shooting at?"

The moment Will's hands were no longer over his head, they started to shiver as though he'd been left out in the cold. He didn't answer Clint's question right away because he was too busy trying to collect himself as the shakes took over more of his system. The effort was like trying to rebuild a house of cards after the bottom had already been knocked out.

"I thought, maybe, it was . . . Eddie," Will said, his eyes brightening a bit once he thought of the name.

Not only could Clint tell that Will was lying, but it was one of the worst lies he'd ever heard. "Try again," he said. "I don't think most children would have believed that one."

"All right. I thought you were Kyle."

"That's better. Now, who's Kyle? Was he the one who brought you that box that's over in the corner there?"

Following Clint's eyes, Will looked over to the box

sitting in the corner. When he looked back to Clint, he nodded.

"What's in the box that's so important?" Clint asked.

"Nothing really."

"Mind if I take a look for myself?"

"Go ahead."

After holstering his gun, Clint stepped over to the box and looked down inside of it. He kept Will in the edge of his field of vision as he rummaged through the contents of the box. It didn't take long for Clint to realize that whatever had caused any of the commotion sure as hell wasn't inside that box. The only things he could find were camping supplies and tools for digging.

"All right now," Clint said, sitting on the edge of the bed. "How about telling me who this Kyle person is."

"His name's Kyle Hammund. He got ahold of me once he found out I had the other half of the map. And before you ask me, I don't know how he knew I had the map. If you want to know that, you might as well ask Eddie, because he's the kind that would sic an animal like Kyle on me."

"Has Kyle threatened you?"

Will laughed once at the question. "That's just for starters. He's threatened me and even my family, who lives in Sacramento. I was hoping to strike out and use my half of the map to take a shot at the gold myself, but he keeps checking in on me right before I leave.

"I even tried to set up an ambush for him the next time he came to town, but it didn't do a bit of good." Will shook his head. "Tell you the truth, I'm too scared to check in on the men I hired because I just know they're dead."

"You hired killers to take this man out?"

"He didn't leave me much choice! After crossing Eddie to get my piece of the map, I intended to get out of here before . . ." Will cut himself off there and looked at Clint with guilt written all over his face.

Clint looked right back at him intently. It was only a matter of seconds before Will couldn't even meet his gaze.

"So you did start this thing between you and Eddie?" Clint asked.

After nodding meekly, Will said, "Eddie's been my partner on a few ventures, but I didn't need him for this. Everything I've heard about this gold is that a man hardly has to dig for it. Just a bit of mining in a shaft that's been abandoned for a few years. It ain't no big deal for an experienced worker like me."

"Or like Eddie," Clint said. "And yet he wasn't the one who wanted to stab his partner in the back just so he didn't have to split the profits with anyone else."

Clint purposely made his words harsh, and his tone harsher, to see what kind of reaction he'd get from Will. That would have been enough to make a man try to defend himself, but not this time. Instead, Will just let his chin drop some more and his head slump down.

Will looked so guilty, ashamed and pathetic at that moment that Clint almost felt sorry for him. Almost, but not quite.

TWENTY-FIVE

"You don't understand," Will grunted. "This could be enough for me to retire on and keep my family supported for the rest of their lives, but not if I had to cut it in half. Once I found out that Eddie didn't even have the whole map, I couldn't bear the thought of having to add another partner."

"Splitting a fortune in gold three ways. Must be rough."

For a moment, Will's eyes shot up and fixed on Clint with a spark of anger. But he was quickly forced to lower his eyes rather than try to dwell on what was already weighing so heavily upon him. "The love of money is the root of all evil. Did you know that?"

Clint nodded. "That's what I've heard."

"I didn't want things to get this far, but even Father Pryde told me that I was doing the right thing, considering my family and how I wanted to provide for them."

"You talked to the priest about this and still went through with it?"

"Yeah. He told me I had nothing to be ashamed of just so long as I used the money the right way. He even said that a man like Eddie didn't deserve something like all that gold and that he was the one sinning for wanting it so bad all for himself."

"And you got all this insight from a man who's been in this town for a month?"

Even though Will didn't say anything right away, Clint saw all the answers he needed written on the man's face. There was a bit of realization there as well as a hint of foolishness.

"But you never thought of that, did you?" Clint asked. "Just so long as you heard what you wanted to hear, why question it, right?"

"Yeah, well, I sure am paying for it now. Kyle keeps dropping in on me and saying he'll find me and kill me if I leave town."

"Dropping in?"

"Yeah. He keeps checking in to make sure I'm here and still have the map, but he hasn't done much more than that, because the law's always been here."

"So why didn't he just take your half of the map from you already?" Clint asked. "I mean, why else would he keep you around?"

"Because he doesn't know where I keep it. Also, I said it would be an easy digging job for a man with experience, and that's me, not him. I'd be dead if Kyle knew his way around a mine. Now that the sheriff's gone, Kyle's here for good, and I'd bet every bit of that gold that he'll kill me as soon as I'm no good to him. Eddie might still finish me off as well. He damn near killed me yesterday."

At that moment, Clint wondered if it would have been so bad if he hadn't been there to step in after all. But it was too late to think about that, just like it was too late for Will to make everything right in his life. All that remained was to straighten out whatever could be saved, and some men weren't so quick to throw down their cards just because the odds didn't favor them.

"So let me get this straight," Clint said, leaning forward and setting one elbow on his knee "You've met with Pryde and talked about all of this and he said that stealing the map was just fine because you had mouths to feed?"

Will nodded.

"And then he went so far as to tell you when Eddie was going to make a move against you."

Will nodded again.

"That's awful nice of him. And how long have you known Father Pryde? It seems like he's going through a lot of trouble to help you out in all of this."

"That's what he does," Will pointed out. "He's a good and decent man. He helps a lot of folks."

"And how did I know you were going to say that?"

Will shrugged and set his chin on the heels of his hands like a scolded child.

After taking a deep breath to clear his head, Clint stood up and said, "All right. Since I've already gotten myself into this, here's what I propose. I'll help you get to this gold and watch your back while you dig it out. That includes keeping an eye out for Eddie, Kyle or anyone else that you still haven't told me about."

Will didn't look very happy about that prospect at all. "Yeah? And how much you asking for your part in this?"

"A third of the profits."

That perked Will up right away. "A third? That's a better deal than Kyle was offering."

"Don't get too excited. Another third still goes to Eddie. It's the least you owe him since he was supposed to be a partner in this as well."

"Aww, hell," Will grumbled.

"No need for the long face," Clint said with a smile. "I can always step aside and let things get a hell of a lot worse."

TWENTY-SIX

When Clint left the boardinghouse, he couldn't stop thinking about one thing: how much he truly couldn't stand a cheater.

Some cheats were truly masters at a difficult craft. There were cardsharps who'd trained themselves to handle aces with a skill that simply had to be admired. They could deal so quickly and so perfectly that the sharpest eyes in the world couldn't spot what was going on.

Men like that may have worked outside the law, but at least they had a genuine talent. Men like those still got themselves killed when they were caught, but they were few and far between and rarely got caught.

Most cheaters were exactly the types of men that made Clint's blood boil. Most cheaters were lazy, stupid and ignorant assholes, which was why killing one was never thought of as too big a deal in most saloons.

They were too lazy to play a game of cards or work for what they wanted, so they tried to cheat to get it. They were too stupid to do much more than stick a card or two up their sleeves and too ignorant to think anyone would notice. In the end, the average cheat was simply an idiot who thought the rest of the world was as dumb as he was.

At least the skilled cheats gave most others the benefit of the doubt and worked hard to cover their tracks. There was no shame in getting beaten by a worthy opponent. No matter how twisted the logic, Clint had to admit that a man who could distinguish a face card by the weight of the ink used to draw it deserved a bit of credit.

He might not deserve the money he stole, but he did deserve some credit, just as an expert gunslinger deserved credit for the skill it took to draw, aim and fire a pistol in a fraction of a second.

But the more he talked to Will Ambrose, the more Clint realized that he was talking to one of the ignorant, lazy kind of cheats.

Will stood to be a rich man even if he had to split the money six ways, but that wasn't enough. Even with half a map the two of them might have been able to find the gold and be done with it, but that wasn't enough either. And if he didn't want to deal with a man like Kyle Hammund, Will could have sold his piece of the map and been done with it, still walking away with a nice profit. But Will was the type of man who'd rather stab a friend in the back, risk his own life and live in fear than just do things the right way.

The more he thought about it, the madder Clint got. He stormed out of the boardinghouse without even acknowledging the gray-haired woman's farewell. The fact of the matter was that Clint hadn't even seen her as he threw open the front door and left the place.

Stepping into the cool air went a long way in easing Clint's nerves. He felt the breeze wash over him and his pulse slow down to something less than the rumble it had been. After he took a moment to savor a few deep breaths, Clint knew that Will's character wasn't the only thing that had gotten him so riled up.

There was also the slight matter of him getting shot at in the hallway. That never put Clint in the best of moods.

It wasn't long before he shook his head at the whole mess and let a smile find its way onto his face. He smiled when he thought about the one thing that he did like about all cheaters.

Once they'd been caught, they were generally very easy to deal with.

Even the dumbest cardsharp knew it was better to go along with whatever deal he was offered rather than face up to the justified wrath of the ones who'd beat him at his own game. Cheaters got themselves killed. That much was common knowledge, and wasn't exclusive to a card table.

Will had done everything he could to get as much of that gold for himself. After cheating his own partner and throwing in with a dangerous gunman, he still wasn't any closer to his goal. In fact, things had been turning around to bite him in the ass, which made him very open to suggestion.

If Clint was more of a cheat himself, he would step in and take Will for everything he was worth, since there couldn't have been a better time. But Clint wasn't a cheat, which meant he was cursed to do things the hard way rather than the way that was easiest or most profitable.

Not that he hadn't had any opportunities to walk in the dark throughout his life. On the contrary, Clint would probably have been able to make a hell of a living if he'd decided to forsake the little things he clung to like morals and high ideals. But there were plenty of advantages to doing things Clint's way. Being able to sleep at night and look at himself in a mirror were the first ones that came to mind.

As he walked along the dirty boards that lined the street, Clint could feel the soothing effects of the fresh air working on his body and soul. Just breathing in the clean, cool purity of the breeze did him a lot of good. It put things into perspective and made him appreciate that he was still alive and well.

In a life where men were after his blood for next to no reason at all, Clint had learned long ago to savor simple things like a crisp breeze and a sunny day.

He also appreciated living by a code that stressed how important it was to leave a place better than when you found it. That went for people as well, and ever since he'd stuck his nose into that fight the other day, Clint had been confronted with the fact that things with those men were about to get a hell of a lot worse. As much as he wished to be otherwise, Clint wasn't the type of man to just let things fall apart when he could help hold them together. It was a simple character flaw, but one that never failed to kick in at the worst times.

Then again, Clint couldn't imagine how boring his life would be without it.

With that in mind, he tipped his hat to a woman leading her little boy by the hand and held the door open for the pair as they walked into the building Clint had been heading for this entire time. At the moment, there were less than half a dozen people in the little church, but Father Pryde was one of them and that was the man Clint had come to see.

TWENTY-SEVEN

"Good day to you, Mr. Adams," Pryde said warmly the moment he saw Clint walk through the church's double doors. "I'm glad to see you on this fine morning."

Clint shook the hand the priest was offering and took a look around at the modest little church. There were some impressive murals painted on the walls, but nothing more elaborate than a landscape with a cross hanging in the sky. The altar was made of finely carved, polished oak and was obviously newer than the rest of the building.

The pews gave off the smell of old lumber and were cracking in several places. The worst areas were probably the ones covered by blankets and quilts, which were draped over the back of a few pews and the seats of some others.

There were two confessionals, which looked more like outhouses since they were battered and worn down so much that one was even listing to the side. The choir box was doubling as a storage space and was half-full with extra chairs and old decorations used for the various holidays.

As Clint looked around, he tried not to react badly to some of the uglier spots and instead smiled while nodding slowly. "This is a nice church," he said. "Simple and traditional."

"Those are kind words," came a voice from behind Pryde. Another man dressed in priest's robes stood up from behind the altar holding a hammer in one hand and nails in the other. "We appreciate the sentiment, but we know our house needs some work. Some of us," he added, holding up the tools, "are just more willing to get splinters in their fingers."

"Alas, I'm not a carpenter," Pryde said. "Clint Adams, this is Father Rayburn. He's been in this parish since the town was founded."

Clint stepped around Pryde and went to the other priest. "I meant no offense. The paintings and that altar really are impressive."

Rayburn was a rotund man with a ring of wiry gray hair starting behind one ear and wrapping around to the back of the other. The top of his head, as well as his brow, was beaded with sweat, but his face didn't seem the least bit tired. Rather, his eyes were bright and his smile was genuine as he accepted Clint's compliment with a subtle nod.

"I helped build this place with these two hands," Rayburn said. "Unfortunately these two hands aren't quite as strong as they used to be."

Clint watched the older priest set down the hammer and nails, noticing that Rayburn's hands looked tougher than leather and strong enough to knock some sense into the most wayward soul. Another thing Clint noticed was the way Rayburn seemed to regard Father Pryde. Along with the tone in his voice, there was something in the older man's eyes that showed there was more that Rayburn wasn't saying. Perhaps it was something he didn't want to say in front of outsiders.

"If you'll excuse me," Rayburn said as he walked around from behind the altar. "It looks like I've got some visitors of my own. It was good to meet you, Mr. Adams. I hope to see you here again for services tomorrow."

"I hope to be here as well, Father Rayburn."

From there, the older priest walked past Clint and Pryde. He opened his arms and welcomed the woman who'd been waiting near the confessionals with her little boy on her lap. They spoke like family members, and Rayburn squatted down to smile warmly into the little boy's face.

Pryde looked at the mother and son for a second before facing Clint. He looked more than a little annoyed when he said, "Sorry about that, Clint. Father Rayburn and I don't get along too well. I think he sees me as a poor replacement for the man who used to work here with him."

"Really? That's a shame."

"He's a good man, though, if a little stuck in his ways. Now, to what do I owe the pleasure of your visit?"

"I checked in with Eddie and Will like you asked."

"Splendid," Father Pryde said. "And how did it go? I hope there were no more confrontations."

"No, nothing like that. There were some shots fired, but as you can see I didn't get in the way of any of them."

"Shots fired? I hope Eddie didn't hurt you."

"Eddie didn't hurt me one bit," Clint said reassuringly. "That's because he wasn't the one who fired at me."

The surprise that came onto Pryde's face was obvious for about a second before it faded away. "So it was Will who tried to shoot you?"

"Actually, he wasn't trying to shoot at me. He mentioned that he was expecting someone else. Apparently this same someone got into town last night, paid Will a visit and scared the daylights out of him."

"Did he know who it was?"

"Kyle Hammund," Clint said the moment Pryde asked the question. He spoke quickly and sharply so the priest wouldn't have any time to brace himself for what he might hear. The tactic worked, in that Clint got a quick peek at the twitch in the corner of Pryde's eye.

It wasn't much, but it said a lot to Clint.

"I've heard of him," Pryde said. "Eddie mentioned him once before things between him and Will came to blows. I believe this Hammund is some kind of hired killer."

"Do you know why he might be in town?" Clint asked. "Or why he came to see Will?"

"I'm not sure."

Pryde was lying. Clint could tell that much the moment those three words came out of the priest's mouth. The signs were hard to read and closely guarded, but they were there and could be spotted by someone with enough experience in dealing with liars. That was an area in which Clint might very well consider himself an expert.

If Pryde thought that Clint was looking at him with anything more than passing interest, he gave no sign. He kept talking, while nervously fidgeting with his hands. "My guess would be that a man like Kyle Hammund would want to get his hands on this gold map that Eddie has been trying to take."

Suddenly, Pryde's eyes widened and he snapped his fingers. "You know what it could be? I think it's very possible that Eddie has hired this Kyle Hammund person to kill Will. He might even be after you now as well."

TWENTY-EIGHT

Clint put some concern in his eyes with expert precision. It was another skill that he'd learned at the poker table and was very useful in keeping the other players off their guard. That subtle show of concern peppered with a trace of worry had made plenty of men think they had Clint right where they wanted him.

Apparently, Father Pryde was thinking that same thing.

"Really?" Clint asked with that barely noticeable shift in his mannerism. "You think he would hire someone to come after both me and Will?"

"He's a desperate man, Mr. Adams. And desperate men do desperate things."

At this point, Clint knew that Pryde wasn't just lying; he was also convinced that his lie was being gobbled up like a fat worm on a hook. Clint recognized that by the victorious gleam in the priest's eyes. The only thing he still couldn't figure out was why that gleam was there in the first place.

Doubting that he would get all the answers he was after in this conversation, Clint decided to try and snag a few anyway. "So what do you think I should do about this?"

Pryde shrugged and shook his head, doing a very good

job of looking troubled by such a disturbing turn of events. "This isn't really my area of specialty, Mr. Adams. If there was any law in town, I might suggest you go to them."

"Well, I could always just leave town. Perhaps things would be better if I just moved on."

"I doubt that," Pryde answered almost a little too quickly. "No man's problems are ever solved by running from them. What did Eddie have to say when you spoke to him? Did he give any indication that he was waiting to hear from anyone?"

"No."

"Did he try to keep you there? Perhaps he was waiting for this Kyle person to arrive."

"That's hard to say," Clint said. "It's possible, I guess. Or it could have been Will that hired him. After all, he was the one who was expecting this gunman to arrive."

"But if he hired him, why would he be shooting at him?"

"Good point." For a few moments, Clint was silent and contemplative. He turned away from Pryde, as if taking some time to mull things over. Instead, he was watching Father Rayburn, who spoke with colorful, friendly gestures to the woman and her child. When the older priest noticed Clint looking his way, Rayburn grew uncomfortable and led the two others outside.

Finally, Clint turned around to face Pryde once again and asked the question he was certain the other man had been waiting for. "What would you suggest, Father?"

Having waited a few moments to seem as though he didn't already have an answer ready, Pryde shrugged and said, "Stay here to face your problems. You seem like a man with good intentions, so the place you could do the most good is here.

"You could take the sheriff's position until he arrives. That way, having a man like this Kyle Hammund in town won't be such a danger. I'm sure someone like you could keep him in line. Perhaps having you around will even show poor Eddie Vale the error of his ways."

"And what about Will?" Clint asked. "He seemed to be doing a bit of straying from the path of the righteous himself."

"I'll speak to him myself. You've already done so much, the least I can do is take some of this burden onto my own shoulders."

"That's real generous of you, Father," Clint said.

"So you'll stay then?"

"Most definitely."

"And the sheriff's job. You'll take that as well?"

"How about I leave that for the man who was voted into that position?"

The disappointment could be seen on Pryde's face, but the priest quickly covered it up with a smile and nodded. "That's fine. I'm sure I speak for this entire community when I say we appreciate every bit of help you're willing to give."

"That's good to know, Father. Now if you'll excuse me, I've got someone else to check in on."

"Going to make sure Eddie stays out of trouble?"

"No. Actually, I wanted to see if I could find this man who visited your friend Will Ambrose. Any idea where Kyle Hammund might be staying?"

Pryde thought about that for a moment and then shook his head. "Not really. You might want to check in on the hotels. There aren't many in town."

"That's funny. Will said he'd talked to you about Hammund. In all that time he didn't mention where the man was staying or how he could be reached?" Clint narrowed his eyes slightly and studied Pryde's face. "That's peculiar indeed."

Another simple tactic, but it worked all the same. Rather than put himself under closer scrutiny, Pryde came up with something to hand over real quickly. "You know something?" the priest suddenly said. "Now that you mention it, I do recall Will telling me about meeting someone at the Gold Coast. There are rooms to rent upstairs, although they're not the best because of the noise and all. Perhaps he was talking about meeting this Hammund person."

"It's a place to start," Clint said, immediately letting up on the pressure his eyes had been putting on the other man. "Thanks for all your help, Father. I'll consider the rest of your proposal and talk to you about it on Sunday."

"Splendid! That's great to hear. Thank you so much, Mr. Adams. You truly are a godsend."

After shaking the priest's hand one more time, Clint turned and left the church. Truth be told, he was in need of some more cool, relaxing air to calm his nerves.

TWENTY-NINE

Stepping out of the church, Clint felt like a teakettle that had been taken off the top of a stove just before the steam whistled out of him. Certain that Pryde was lying to him, he'd done his best to get something useful out of the priest by acting as though he was swallowing up everything that was being fed to him.

Not only did it tax Clint's nerves, but it made him want to break apart Pryde's game by coming right out and saying that he wasn't being fooled at all. Just because Clint understood liars and cheats didn't make it any easier to deal with them. If he just wanted to get to the gold, it would have been a lot easier. But Clint had a gnawing suspicion that there were lives at stake as well.

If nothing else, Clint was certain that Eddie Vale was being set up to take a fall, and if Clint wasn't the one who took him down, there would be someone else less willing to question the lines fed to them. Once the stakes got that high, Clint knew there was no cashing out. It was either follow through or let blood get spilled, and if he walked away before seeing it through, Clint knew it could very well be innocent blood.

Just like before, the cool air did him a world of good.

Clint stood in front of the church and immediately found the spot where Father Rayburn was talking to the young woman and her son. They appeared to be in the midst of saying their goodbyes and there were smiles on all three of their faces.

The smile on Father Rayburn's face lasted right up to the point when he saw that Clint was looking at him.

After one last wave, the older priest parted company with the woman and child so he could head toward the church. Although he didn't look at Clint, he didn't look away either.

"Excuse me," Clint said while walking forward to intercept the priest before he got to the church's front step. "Excuse me, Father Rayburn."

It wasn't until the second time Clint spoke that the priest halted and glanced in his direction. His face was somber and colder than the breeze that enveloped both him and Clint. "Yes? What is it?"

"I wonder if I could have a moment of your time."

"There is still much work that needs to be done inside. Perhaps you'd rather talk with Father Pryde. He usually has plenty of free time on his hands."

"Actually, I was hoping to speak with you. Since I've already heard Father Pryde's take on matters, I'd like to hear the truth."

Father Rayburn didn't even flinch at that. Instead, he studied Clint a little harder before a faint smile crept over his face. "You think the young father is lying to you about something?"

"No," Clint said. "I know it for a fact that he's lying. And something tells me that you know it, too."

"And what would give you that idea?"

"Well, a blind man could see that you don't care for him as a person. I'll bet that there's plenty of folks in this town who feel the same way. Maybe that's why you brought that young woman out here in the cold to talk rather than stay inside the church and out of the wind."

Rayburn lifted his head to a breeze as it passed by, feeling the cold embrace as it swept through his entire body. When he looked back at Clint, he nodded and started walking toward a small fenced-in cemetery beside the church. "Take a walk with me for a moment. I find it's easier to talk in private outside the confines of man-made walls."

Falling into step next to Rayburn, Clint waited until they'd put some distance between themselves and the church before speaking again. "You didn't seem surprised when I said Father Pryde was lying to me."

"That's because I wasn't. I've heard plenty of complaints about him from others in town, but none of them have been so blunt."

"You have your own concerns about him as well, don't you?"

"Of course. And I had plenty of concerns about you as well, since you and Pryde seemed to be getting along so well."

"You knew who I was?" Clint asked. "And what I was doing in town?"

"It's a small town, Mr. Adams. I didn't know exactly what brought you to Richwater, but I knew that Pryde had your ear. Some of the others were telling me about you and your . . . let's just say . . . less than savory reputation. I was beginning to think the worst."

"And that would be?"

"Another funeral in the near future."

"Let me guess what the name on that headstone would be. Eddie Vale?"

Rayburn nodded, looking down at a nearby headstone as though he already saw those letters etched in stone. "Pryde may be subtle as he goes about his activities, but I spend a lot of time with him. How did you draw such a conclusion?"

"You mean how could I know such a thing and really be new in town?" Clint asked.

"Forgive my tone, Mr. Adams. Consider it caution rather than outright suspicion."

"You have a right to either one, Father. The answer is that a man doesn't live too long with a reputation as unsavory as mine without being a good judge of character. Every time I talked to Father Pryde, he directed every bad sentiment toward Eddie and made Will Ambrose out to be some kind of poor, helpless victim. I was there when those two were about to kill each other and they both looked mad as hell, but neither one struck me as particularly innocent. More than that, I don't like anyone thinking they can lead me around by the nose. It just rubs me the wrong way."

The cemetery wasn't very big and they were already walking past the last row of headstones. Rayburn waited until they were out of the burial grounds before coming to a stop. He gazed out onto an expanse of open land and said, "I felt the same way, Mr. Adams. The first time I met Father Pryde, he just rubbed me the wrong way. For the first week he was in town, I couldn't even tell you why.

"You're not the only good judge of character," Rayburn said, glancing over at Clint. "I served in this town long enough and have heard enough confessions to be able to read between the lines. I listen, Mr. Adams. That's what I do. And that includes listening to things I've heard about you."

Suddenly, Clint felt as though he'd stepped into the glare of an overly lit stage. "Uh-oh. Do I even want to ask about what you've heard?"

"Probably not. Suffice it to say that every last thing I heard had you fighting a good fight and landing on the right side more often than not. People like to stress the grisly details, but I listen for the consistencies rather than conjecture."

"It doesn't make me feel any better to hear you talking like such a lawyer."

Laughing, Rayburn said, "I think you're a man of action with a good heart. It sounds to me like you help people in need even at the expense of your own safety. That was why it angered me to see you working with someone like Father Pryde."

"Would you like to hear something I've noticed?" Clint asked.

"Certainly."

"It seems to make your stomach twist to say the word 'Father' in front of Pryde's name."

"Very observant, but I would worry less about him at the moment and more about the men that do take his word as gospel."

"Really? Anyone in particular?"

"Kyle Hammund would be a great place to start."

THIRTY

"I'd like to tell you that this is about more than just gold, Mr. Adams," Father Rayburn said. "But that's just not the case."

"The love of money," Clint said, which brought an appreciative grin to Rayburn's face.

"That's correct. The root of all evil. And it couldn't be more true than it is here. I fear that the only time Father Pryde shows any interest in his flock is when it involves a story about that damned map that Will and Eddie have been fighting over."

"You think it's genuine?"

"That doesn't matter. What does matter is that enough people believe it to be genuine and will therefore kill for it. There has already been cheating, lying and stealing, so murder is next. I was afraid that day had come already, but you showed up to put a stop to it.

"I would have come to thank you myself, but Pryde was already there. Once I saw that you were taking him into your confidence, I thought that you might be the man I was worried about."

"You were worried about someone?"

"I'd heard periodically of a man coming into town. A

gunfighter. Finally, I alerted the sheriff and told him to find this man or there would be blood spilled."

"If Pryde had his way, I would be the sheriff right about now," Clint said. "He's been after me to take the job since I got here."

"That's not surprising. The sheriff gets along with Pryde as well as I do, which isn't well at all. The sheriff came to me alone and I helped him narrow down the area to search for this gunfighter I'd heard so much about."

"What was this gunfighter supposed to do?"

"He had the rest of the map," Rayburn answered. "And he wanted to piece the whole thing together so they could go after that gold." The priest shook his head wearily. "So much grief over a deposit of metal. It truly seems ridiculous when you think about it."

"No argument here."

"You may think this is silly, Mr. Adams, but I believe that you were sent here for a purpose. Talking to you now, I am even more convinced that you're here in this town to keep two good souls from killing each other over the love of money.

"Deep down in their hearts, I don't think Will and Eddie want to fight any longer. I can see Father Pryde encouraging them only when it involves one hurting the other."

"You mean Will hurting Eddie?"

"That's right. He steps in to protect only Will, and that's because Will was closest to Pryde ever since he arrived in town a month ago. He's tried to get Will to do something to protect himself, but the truth of the matter is that the whole thing would go away if Pryde would step back and let the two friends clear it up on their own."

"Do you think Pryde wants Eddie dead?" Clint asked.

Rayburn fell silent for a few moments, until he finally let his eyes lower so that he was looking at the ground, as if seeing a fresh burial plot at his feet. "Possibly. He wants him out of his way, I know that much for sure."

"How can you be certain?"

"Because he lives in the next room over from me. I've heard the things he's said to Will when the poor man came to Pryde for council, and I can see the intensity in Pryde's face when he talks about it. I've heard him talk to Eddie as well, and the only thing he can say is for him to turn himself in or step aside for the sake of the law or for friendship.

"Either way, it's always the same. He tells Eddie to give up and Will to keep fighting. Then I heard about a gunfighter coming, and later I heard about you coming. I saw how Pryde treated you and thought you might be the man to put this matter to a close."

Clint stood with the priest for another minute or two as both men let their thoughts settle inside of them like dirt that had been kicked up at the bottom of a lake. Once the waters were clear again, Clint glanced over his shoulder toward the church.

Sure enough, Father Pryde was standing next to the building, watching them. When Clint saw the younger priest wave at him, he responded with a single nod and turned back to face Rayburn.

"He's watching us, isn't he?" the older priest asked without having to look back to where Pryde was standing.

"Yep."

"He knows what I think of him."

Clint smirked and said, "Well, it doesn't seem like you go to great lengths to hide it."

"I guess I don't. Is it a sin for a man like me to hold another in such contempt?"

"Only if he doesn't deserve it, Father."

Rayburn took a deep breath and straightened up. When he looked at Clint, he wore an easy smile that would have put anyone's mind at ease. Anyone who didn't know better, that is.

"So what do you think of all this, Mr. Adams? It's a lot to hear from someone you've just met. Admittedly, it's not even your problem. I appreciate you listening to me."

"No problem, Father. Sometimes, that's what I do as well." Clint returned the priest's smile and could tell that Rayburn was still sizing him up. Before, it seemed as though the older priest wasn't sure about him. Although there was still some doubt in those weary eyes, Clint could also tell that he'd gained some real ground.

"If tensions are running as high as you say," Clint told him, "and this other gunfighter is in town, then things are going to be moving a lot quicker. Me being here might have just sped things up."

"Good. The sooner all this bloody business is over, the better."

"I need to know a few things first, like where the sheriff went to go look for this Kyle Hammund. I also need to know where Hammund is now. Anything else you can tell me would be helpful. You think you could do that for me?"

Rayburn nodded. "Most folks are still more comfortable with me over Pryde. I can tell you everything I know now and find out the rest later."

"Good. One thing I can tell you for certain right now is that I will bring this matter to a close."

THIRTY-ONE

Clint found out a lot of things in a short amount of time. Once Father Rayburn had made his decision to take him into his confidence, he spelled out the entire situation for Clint down to the last detail. As he listened, Clint decided what he needed to do and in which order.

First on his list was to see about tracking down the town's law, since the sheriff was still a no-show and his remaining deputies were comfortable enough sitting on their hands until he arrived. Next, Clint listened to every last thing Rayburn had heard about Kyle Hammund, starting with where the gunfighter might be found while in town and how long he'd been waiting there.

Besides a description that matched the one given by the woman Clint spoke to at Will's boardinghouse, Rayburn mentioned talk of some trouble at a feed store in town involving a similar man. The more Clint heard, the more convinced he became that time was running out before something bad happened in the streets of Richwater.

After getting to the livery and saddling up Eclipse, Clint rode out of town, headed in the same direction as the sheriff had gone several days before. Even though the lawman traveled frequently between many small towns in the area, everyone seemed to have expected him back some time ago.

That was why Clint decided to track down that man first. Once he caught up with the sheriff, he would have a better idea of where to go next and how much of the fight brewing within Richwater was going to land on his shoulders. The moment he had Eclipse pointed in the right direction, Clint snapped his reins and held on as the Darley Arabian stallion thundered out of town as though he'd been shot from a cannon.

On his way out of Richwater, Clint passed directly in front of the Gold Coast Saloon. As he raced on by, he glanced over at the building, turning his eyes up to the row of windows on the second floor. According to Father Rayburn, that was where Kyle Hammund would be found. Since it shouldn't take more than the day and a good part of the night to catch up to the sheriff, Clint focused on that task alone.

Hopefully, Hammund would think that Clint was still somewhere in town and wouldn't be so quick to make any sudden moves. It was one of the times that Clint relied on his reputation, and it always made him uncomfortable to count on something so vague. But all he needed was for Hammund to stay put for the day. After that, Clint himself would be back in town to make some moves of his own.

And if everything went well, he wouldn't be alone when he came riding back into town.

Kyle had been sitting in the rickety chair in his room over the Gold Coast for about ten minutes. Every second of that time had been spent looking out the window and idly polishing the gold-plated handle of his revolver. He felt the soft surface of the gold beneath the cloth in his hand as his eyes wandered over the street outside the saloon.

It never ceased to amaze him how much one small town

looked like another. Each one had different names on the buildings, but that was about the only thing he could use to tell them apart. They all were dirty and shabby excuses for settlements, populated with dimwitted sheep who were too lazy to move into a city or see another part of the world.

He shook his head and smiled at how stupid those people walking on the street below truly were. They didn't have a clue that they were missing so much. Or maybe they just didn't care. Either way, it didn't really matter to Kyle Hammund, since he was only thinking about it to pass the time.

People could be as stupid as they wanted and that was just fine with him. In fact, he made a decent living off of other people's stupidity, as well as their pathetic fears. He thought about the sheriff that was supposed to be riding into town at any moment as an example. That made him smile.

His smile grew even wider when he spotted a familiar face coming up the walkway and stopping directly across the street. She was a short girl with long, wavy blond hair and a curvy figure accentuated by a form-fitting pink dress. She looked up at Kyle's window, saw him smiling and gave him a smile of her own in return.

Kyle was more than happy to let her think that he was smiling at her. After all, didn't most people think every last thing in the world was directed at them? Fucking idiots.

It was then that he spotted another familiar person as he thundered down the street riding a sleek, impressive stallion. Kyle had heard that Clint Adams was in town, but now it seemed as though the great Gunsmith was on his way out.

If he was smart, Adams would keep riding. If Adams returned, he wouldn't just be another idiot.

He'd be a dead fucking idiot.

THIRTY-TWO

She knocked on the door in a quick, pattering rhythm. The moment her hand was available, she slid her fingers through her long blond hair and gathered it together to pull over one shoulder the way she knew he liked it. Listening to the heavy steps approaching from the other side of the door, she made sure her new pink dress was situated just right and that every last hook was in its place.

When she looked up again, she saw the door open, and waiting for her on the other side was the gaunt face of the man she'd been thinking about. "Hello, Kyle," she said. "Can I come in?"

Hammund stepped aside and watched her closely as she sauntered into the room. Just like the last time he'd seen her, the blonde's innocence didn't hold up well at all under closer inspection. She knew he was watching her and shifted her hips accordingly. Every move she made affected him in some way, right down to the slow turn as she swiveled around to look at him over her shoulder.

After shutting the door, Kyle came up behind her and placed his hands on her hips. As he moved in closer to her, he pressed his hips against the smooth, generous curve of her backside and felt her push back against him with a little grind of her own.

"I was watching you through my window," he whispered.

She smiled and leaned her head back against his shoulder. "I know. I saw you smiling at me." When she spoke, she sounded sweet and breathy. She even kept that innocent tone in her voice when she told him, "I was thinking about coming up here and fucking you the moment I saw your face."

"Yeah? Is that what you were thinking?"

He could feel her heart beating faster as he moved his hands over her stomach and chest. When she pulled in a deep breath, her breasts swelled against the palms of his hands, straining at the delicate fabric of her dress.

"I've been thinking about you since the first time you came into town," she said. "Ever since the first time you touched me, I never wanted your hands to be off my body. Sometimes I just can't stand it when you're not here."

As Kyle slid one hand over her midsection, he reached between her legs and pressed his fingers against the warm spot there. She clenched her eyes shut and moaned softly, pushing her hips forward and opening her legs so he could get easier access.

Brushing his mouth lightly against her ear, he told her, "I think you're the only person in this town that likes it when I'm here."

Her smile was wide and sensual when she thought about that. "I know. Most folks never see you coming. And the ones that do talk about you like you're some kind of monster." Suddenly, her eyes shot open and she twisted herself around so she could look at him better, while still allowing him to fondle her through the dress.

"Were you at Matt's store yesterday?" she asked.

After a moment of looking deeply into her eyes, Kyle nodded.

Seeing that, the blonde shuddered slightly. Part of her was reacting to the thought of what he'd done and the other was responding to Kyle's probing fingers, which rubbed her pussy through the layers of her skirts. "Did those men they found shoot at you?" she asked.

Kyle nodded as he moved both hands up over her body to cup her breasts, squeezing them tightly as he pushed his hips harder against her firm buttocks. Even through the material of her dress, Kyle could feel the blonde's nipples becoming erect. When he reached down between her legs again, he could feel she was getting hotter there as well.

Suddenly, she moved away from him and turned around. Her eyes wandered hungrily over his body, lingering on the growing bulge in his crotch. Now it was her turn to let her hands roam over him. She teased him with fingers tracing lightly over his groin, but focused mainly on opening his shirt and sliding her fingers inside.

Kyle savored the feel of her fingers on his skin and the way she slowly pulled the shirt away from his body. "You like hearing about things like that, Angelica?"

The blonde nodded slowly, not trying to hide the excitement in her eyes. "You know I do. There's nobody else in town who would stand up to people the way you do."

"What did you hear about what happened?"

"Just that some men were shot dead at Matt's store. The deputy who checked on it is keeping it quiet, but I hear that even Matt Anderson is dead."

Kyle could tell by the way she looked at him that Angelica was curious about what happened and was fishing for more information. He gave her a subtle nod, which was enough to confirm the rumor that she'd been talking about.

Seeing that, Angelica's body trembled with excitement and her fingers worked to pull open Kyle's pants. She barely had them open before reaching in to stroke his erect penis. "You killed them all?"

Kyle nodded again.

Angelica's eyes widened as she lowered herself to her knees and slowly moved her hands over his stomach and groin. After pulling his pants down a bit more, she looked up into his face, opened her mouth and put the tip of his cock between her lips.

Her hands moved down along his thighs and up again as her tongue slid back and forth on the sensitive underside of his rigid penis. Angelica's lips didn't close tightly around his shaft until her hands made their way up to his gun belt. The moment she could feel the bullets there, she let out a soft purring sound, while taking him all the way into her mouth.

Kyle felt his legs shake a bit as her lips and tongue worked expertly on him. He slid his fingers through her golden hair, making sure she didn't pull too far back or slide him out of her mouth until he was ready. He held her right where she was when she began to swirl her tongue around the tip of his cock before slowly moving her lips along its length.

Just when he felt his pleasure start to boil over, Kyle eased her away from him and helped her to her feet. She smiled widely, then slowly licked her lips as he began pulling the dress off of her body.

THIRTY-THREE

Angelica's body was soft and compact. She was a short young woman who carried herself as though she towered over most everybody else. Because of that, she didn't look away from Kyle for a moment as he undressed her, and instead helped him by moving her shoulders or shifting her weight at the proper times. When she was naked in front of him, she slowly moved her hands up over her round hips and along her sides until she could cup her breasts.

Her pink nipples were already hard with excitement, but she pinched them between her fingers because she liked the way it felt and didn't care if anyone was watching her or not. Her stomach moved in and out with quick, deep breaths as he got closer. The moment Kyle stood still, she practically ripped the clothes off of him, her fingernails scraping his flesh in the process.

Once again, she lowered herself onto her knees. This time, she reached for the gold-handled pistol that lay in the holster near Kyle's feet. Her fingers didn't even touch the glittering yellow grip of the weapon before Kyle swatted it away.

She didn't seem offended by the gesture. On the contrary, she seemed even more excited to have crossed into some sort of forbidden territory. "Those men you shot," she whispered, still kneeling in front of him. "Did you do it with that gun?"

Kyle was bending at the waist so he could reach the weapon on the floor. From there, he looked into the blonde's eyes and smiled. He took the weapon from its holster, took hold of Angelica by one arm and lifted her onto her feet. All it took was a strong shove and Angelica landed on the bed with a huffing exhale. He crawled next to her and lay on his side, and she immediately got close enough to rub the soft thatch of hair between her legs against his stiff column of flesh.

"You like thinking about things like that, don't you?" Kyle asked as he slowly rubbed the gun's barrel against her bare shoulder.

Looking down at the firearm that was in the killer's hand, Angelica let out a shuddering breath which sounded close to an orgasm. "Y-yes."

Kyle pressed the side of the pistol against her belly, touching the gold to her skin before easing the end of the barrel over her hip. "And what if I told you I did kill those men with this gun? Would that scare you?"

Her breathing was still coming in gasps and her body squirmed against the mattress. She didn't move as though she wanted to get away, but instead seemed to be aching to feel more of what was driving her so crazy. "It wouldn't scare me," she said. After a moment's pause, she added, "Well, maybe a little."

"But you'd still like it, wouldn't you?" Kyle asked as he turned the gun over and slid it along the inside of one of her thighs.

Angelica reflexively opened her legs for him and arched her back against the bed. The movement lifted her perky breasts into the air and tightened her already flat stomach. "Yes," she moaned. "I like it."

Kyle moved on top of her, settling between her legs and moving the gun up her side and along one arm. The moment his stiff cock brushed against the damp lips of her vagina, Angelica reached down and fit him inside of her, groaning with satisfaction as he slid inside.

Her legs were strong, and one of them wrapped around him, pulling him in more with a foot against the small of his back. The other leg rubbed against Kyle's as he thrust deeply into her with one powerful motion.

The blonde's pussy tightened around him, enveloping him in her warm, moist skin. Kyle felt his cock stiffen even more, but refrained from letting himself go and give in to the urges that flew through his mind and body. Instead, he savored the way she reacted to the feel of the gun against her body.

She flinched whenever she felt the cold barrel touch her someplace new, but smiled when she realized what it was that she was feeling. Her breath caught in the back of her throat for a moment when she felt the top of the barrel press against the side of her head. Opening her eyes, she found Kyle staring straight down at her with a wild spark in his gaze.

"I could kill you right now," he said in a voice that sounded more like a hiss than a whisper.

She nodded slowly, shifting her hips so that she could slide him in and out of her even with him remaining completely still. "I know you could," she told him. "That's why I want to feel as good as I can right this moment."

Hearing that, Kyle smirked a bit before easing his thumb over the hammer and slowly pulling it back until the distinct metallic click sounded through the room. He watched her face closely, looking for whatever change might come over her.

There was no fear in Angelica's eyes. There wasn't even any anxiousness. Instead, the blonde pushed her head back against the mattress even harder and turned her face into the gun barrel, until the cold steel was pressed against her temple. From there, she looked at Kyle, wrapped her leg tighter around him and worked her hips even harder back and forth.

If he didn't do anything at all, Kyle would have been worked up into an orgasm in a matter of seconds. Her pussy was clenching him tightly and she pumped her hips back and forth in an insistent rhythm as though she was truly savoring her final moments on earth.

"You really are crazy, aren't you?" Kyle said as he eased the hammer down and tossed the gun onto the floor beside the bed.

"For you? Maybe a little." Angelica slowed down her pace only once Kyle had lifted himself onto his knees, grabbed hold of her hips with both hands and begun thrusting in and out of her. She wriggled a little to help him hit the right spots inside of her while moving her hands over her breasts and then through her hair.

Lifting her backside up off the bed, Kyle pumped into her harder with every thrust until both of their breaths started coming in sharp, loud bursts. He watched as Angelica arched her back and let out a grunting moan. Her breasts shook with the rhythm of their lovemaking and her nipples were fully erect.

Soon, Kyle felt his orgasm coming and grabbed onto her with all his strength. His last several thrusts were almost savage, but Angelica merely spread her legs open wider to receive them. In fact, once she felt that he was about to explode inside of her, she began to climax as well.

When Kyle stopped, Angelica pumped her own hips back and forth again until every one of her muscles tensed at the height of her pleasure. Only then did she let her backside touch the mattress again and her legs loosen enough for Kyle to get free.

With the tingles of her orgasm still working their way

through her skin, she rolled onto her stomach and let one arm fall over the side of the bed. Her hand wasn't even halfway to the pistol laying on the floor before Kyle grabbed her by the wrist and held her in place.

"You know better than that," he warned.

"But I want to touch it."

"You did touch it. Don't push me any further."

Sensing the stern tone in his voice, Angelica rolled over until her breasts were brushing against Kyle's chest. "Then let me see you use it."

The blonde's body felt soft and warm against his, but Kyle didn't have any trouble keeping his mind on the subject at hand. "What are you talking about?"

"You've still got business in town; otherwise you'd already be gone. I want to see you pull the trigger. That would just drive me out of my head."

"I'll bet it would, and I would love to see that," Kyle said truthfully. "But you're right about one thing. I have a job to do. Business is business."

"Then let me help you."

Kyle's first impulse was to dismiss the idea. Then he thought for a moment and a smile slid over his lips. "You know something? I just might have something for you to do. It could be dangerous, though. Does that scare you?"

"Yes," Angelica replied, her eyes flashing with excitement. "A little."

THIRTY-FOUR

Eclipse thundered over the landscape like a pure force of nature. The Darley Arabian's hooves pounded against the soil in a constant barrage, fueled by burning muscles which sent steam from the stallion's nostrils. Richwater was a few miles behind them by now, but Eclipse showed no sign of wanting to slow down. On the contrary, he seemed to be reveling in the thrill of running flat-out without a care in the world.

As much as Clint loved to let the big horse get his fill of exercise, he wasn't exactly sure how much farther they had to go. He'd been told a general area to search for the sheriff, but that area was several miles in diameter. Even a horse as strong as Eclipse could burn himself out if a rider wasn't careful, and the chill in the air would only bite deeper as the day wore on into night.

Clint pulled back slightly on the reins, putting just enough tension on the leather straps to communicate his intentions. That was all Eclipse needed before easing out of a full gallop. Clint's ears were still ringing as the horse's steps lost some of their power, making Clint appreciate how a bullet must feel after being shot from a rifle. Even though his innards were still rattling inside of him, he had to admit that it was exhilarating. In fact, it took him a moment to realize that he was practically grinning from ear to ear.

The trail stretched out before him, winding through rises and disappearing over a set of rolling hills. According to Father Rayburn, that was the direction that the sheriff had gone in search of the gunfighter that was supposedly on his way to stir up trouble in town. Since that gunfighter had already arrived and there was still no sign of the lawman, Clint had to assume that trouble had found the sheriff instead.

Until that moment, the country around him had been fairly open and easy to search as he and Eclipse bolted through the miles. But now he could pick out more places to hide amid the little caves and gulleys on either side of the trail, so Clint thought it best to look over them more carefully. Besides that, he figured Eclipse was going to be racing back into town once he found what he'd been looking for, so there was no sense in burning the stallion out too much so early.

Clint reached into one of his saddlebags to retrieve the spyglass he kept there. The telescope was dented in spots and smelled a bit like tarnished copper as he raised it to his eye, but the lenses were still in fine shape. Through them, he scanned a few dark shapes he'd spotted that caught his attention.

With Eclipse still moving at a steady pace, the best Clint could do was get a quick look at the shapes in the distance through the jostling telescope. That was enough for him to tell that the first few of those shapes were nothing more than clumps of dirty rocks or the occasional rotting stump.

By the fourth time he lifted the glass to his eye, Clint had gotten pretty good at compensating for the stallion's movement and steadying his own hand. The shapes that had caught his attention were scattered over a large area within a clearing less than a quarter of a mile away. At first glance, he thought they were more logs, but he managed to make out one particular detail that made a big difference.

"Whoa, boy," Clint said while pulling back on Eclipse's reins. The Darley Arabian was reluctant to break his stride, but complied with the command without question. As soon as he came to a stop, Eclipse lowered his head and pulled up some grass near his feet.

Clint picked out the spot he wanted to see in the distance and peered through the spyglass. A bit of adjusting was all it took for him to focus on that particular detail he'd seen.

Even though the larger shapes looked like logs, there had to be something else there. After all, logs didn't wear hats.

If it hadn't been sitting in the middle of a batch of pale weeds, Clint might not have even been able to see the hat laying there. As it was, the hat stuck out like a sore thumb, propped up and waving in the breeze as though it had been planted there to attract attention. If that was the case, it certainly had done its job.

Taking a few more moments to look closely at the area near the hat, Clint saw that there were indeed logs laying in the grass. He didn't let it go at that, however, and studied as much as he could through the lenses. Sure enough, he picked out another detail: boots sticking out from the end of one log.

He nodded grimly to himself while dropping the telescope back into his saddlebag. Steering Eclipse toward that clearing, Clint snapped the reins and charged forward. Even though he didn't know exactly what he was going to find, Clint was pretty sure he wouldn't like it.

The Darley Arabian covered the distance in no time flat. Before they got too close, Clint brought the stallion to a stop and swung down from the saddle. He didn't bother tying off the reins, since he knew Eclipse wouldn't go anywhere. Besides that, Clint was too distracted by the shapes on the ground to think about such mundane precautions.

From a distance, it had appeared as though the boots were sticking out of one end of the log. Now that he was up close, Clint could tell that there wasn't anything inside the log, but rather something wedged behind and underneath it.

Clint stepped forward and into the clearing. His right hand stayed low at his side, ready to draw the Colt at the first hint of danger. His nerves were drawn taut within him, making it feel like the hackles were raising up on the back of his neck.

Most of that tension came from the smell of blood which was heavy in the air. The distinctive coppery stench tainted a breeze that had died down, as if in respect for the dead strewn about the area.

Walking carefully between the logs, Clint looked around and counted the bodies. There were three that he could see right away. Reluctantly, he put his toe against one log and rolled it away from him and was almost knocked out by the stench of rotting flesh.

"Jesus Christ," Clint whispered. "What the hell happened here?"

THIRTY-FIVE

After taking a few breaths to clear his head, Clint squatted down to get a closer look at the ground. The dirt was compact and cold, which made tracks easier to spot. Even though he wasn't the best tracker in the world, Clint had eyes and enough common sense to interpret some of what he saw.

First of all, it was obvious that the men had made camp in that clearing, since there were remains of a fire in the middle of the group of logs. Second, Clint could tell that the men were probably taken by surprise, since there weren't a whole lot of tracks more than a foot or two from each of the bodies.

Third, he knew the men had been picked off over the course of a few minutes, since a few of them had had enough time to reload their guns. The empty shell casings around two of the bodies told Clint that much. And finally, whoever had killed them knew someone would be looking for the bodies.

It didn't take a brilliant tracker to figure that last part out, since the bodies had all been stuffed out of sight like so much garbage. The corpses were mostly beneath the logs, and one of them had only been pushed down into the dirt as a log was rolled on top of him. Clint figured that out when he nearly tripped over the rut in the ground where the log had obviously been before.

Clint was used to seeing dead bodies. It wasn't something that he was proud of, but he'd been around long enough to see more than his fair share. What made his stomach turn was the way those bodies had been treated. Whoever had stashed them away did so with as much respect as would be given to stamping out a fire.

The killer was also one hell of a shot. Walking around to each body in turn, Clint saw that most of them were shot through the skull. In fact, all but one of them had a hole punched through the forehead like a third eye. It struck Clint as something more than a killing shot.

Those bullet holes were signatures, and the killer was signing his name to each one from some sense of morbid pride.

There was only one more thing that Clint wanted to look for. As much as he wanted to just get the sight of those carcasses out of his mind, he went to each one in turn and searched the clothes. The bodies were all fairly fresh, and the only thing that kept the stench from knocking Clint over was the fact that it was still fairly cold and they were out of the sun.

The dead flesh felt like beef that had been stored in a cold chophouse. It was on one of the bigger of the dead men that Clint found what he'd been searching for. Pinned to the corpse's jacket was a dented badge marking him as a sheriff.

Clint took the badge from the man and walked over to place it in a saddlebag. He also took out a small shovel used mostly for digging out fire pits and walked back to the clearing. If he'd had more time, Clint would have buried each of the bodies himself. But since he needed to get back to town as quickly as possible, he pushed the logs away and loosened enough dirt to cover the bodies.

When he was done, Clint went back to Eclipse and was about to climb into the saddle when he spotted something else. Actually, it seemed as though Eclipse had spotted it, since the stallion was nervously fussing with a spot in the ground covered with some tall grass. Clint walked over to that spot and found yet another body laying there.

This body was different from the rest, not only in the way it was dressed, but in the placement of its wound. It had no signature like the others, but a bullet hole in the back instead. There was no badge, but all Clint had to see was the clothes on the body to know it was no lawman.

Kneeling down to the corpse, he reached for something laying next to the body. It was a book, and Clint didn't feel the first sparks of rage until he read what was inscribed on the inside of the front cover.

The anger had been something building up inside of him the entire time he'd gone about his morbid task. It was a kind of rage that burned within his chest like a pile of smoldering coals. Until now, Clint had been certain that there was probably a lot going on in Richwater that he didn't know about. Every town had its ghosts, just like every man had his demons.

Will Ambrose and Eddie Vale might have had a history that had been leading up to this point for some time, and Clint had only come in to see a part of the story. Every question he asked about the situation would shed a different light on the whole matter, and until this point, Clint had been willing to sift through as much of it as he could.

But the anger inside his gut didn't have anything to do with having to deal with Will or Eddie or even Father Pryde. The anger came from seeing human beings treated like cattle in a slaughterhouse. It was obvious that whoever had killed those men didn't lose a moment's rest about it.

The shots were clean and precise. The kills were even marked with the killer's own personal seal.

What Clint felt didn't have anything to do with the gold that was at stake, either. As far as he was concerned, he didn't want any part of something that had brought so much death. He'd rather be poor than give in to the root of the evil he'd witnessed.

Clint took one last look at the piles of loose dirt before steering Eclipse in the other direction. Someone would come back to that spot and bury those lawmen properly. He vowed to make that happen even if he had to come back with a shovel and do it himself.

But first, he had to pay a visit to the man responsible for the lives that had ended in that clearing. Only then would the burning in Clint's soul cool down.

THIRTY-SIX

Despite the fact that Kyle Hammund wasn't completely decked out in black as he was when he'd arrived, he still seemed to carry a darkness about him that other folks could see. It was almost as if he had been in the shadows for so long that it tainted his very soul.

Locals who had a friendly smile on their faces when they saw someone walking their way quickly turned to look down once they got a glimpse at Hammund's eyes. Kyle saw the fear he inspired and tipped his hat as a reply. He kept right on walking, taking strong, easy steps, as though he had all the time in the world.

The sun was low on the horizon and soon all the light would be gone from the sky. Having spent most of the day either in his room with Angelica or downing whiskey at the Gold Coast, Kyle was in fairly good spirits.

And why shouldn't he be?

Soon, he would have everything he came for, and not too much longer after that, he would be rich as well. That was enough to put a smile on anyone's face, even if they were as unaccustomed to smiling as Kyle Hammund.

The closer he got to the boardinghouse where Will was staying, the more people recognized him and got out of his way. Kyle walked through the middle of the opening he created, which led right up to the front door of the boardinghouse. He pulled the door open and stepped inside, noticing the startled jump of the old woman who'd been standing there.

"Wh-what do you want?" the gray-haired woman asked.

"Just paying another visit here, that's all. Is Will upstairs?"

"Yes, but I don't want any more trouble!"

"There wasn't even any trouble last time I was here, so don't worry about it now."

The older woman's eyes widened and she moved as though she was about to step forward, but immediately stopped herself from getting closer. "I don't want no more shooting up there. It doesn't matter who you are or what you're doing, this is my livelihood and I can't have no men filling it full of holes. Someone could've been hurt."

Kyle listened to her tirade with a mildly amused expression. When he saw that she was finished, he looked toward the stairs and studied them carefully. He couldn't see much of the upper floor, apart from what he could glimpse through the entryway at the top of the steps, but it seemed as though there wasn't much movement.

The old woman started to say something else, but Kyle stopped her with a quickly extended hand, which he waved in a gentle warning. "Shhh," he said. "That's enough out of you for right now."

But the gray-haired woman had already gotten herself riled up enough to start, so she seemed determined to finish. "By God, I swear I've had my fill of you types who think they can just—"

Kyle's hand snapped forward until he clasped it over the old woman's mouth. He took another step toward her, keeping his face calm and only mildly aggressive. "Don't make me tell you again, ma'am." As he gave the warning, he flicked open the side of his coat to reveal the gold-handled gun at his side. "You said there was shooting up there?"

She began to make a sound, but merely nodded once she saw that Kyle wasn't about to take his hand away.

"When did that happen?" he asked.

Once Kyle slowly pulled his hand back, the woman let out an anxious breath. "Earlier today."

"Who was shooting?"

"I . . . I thought it was you."

Kyle shook his head. "Hate to disappoint you, but you're wrong about that. Try again."

"Another man came here to visit Will," she told him. "He went up the stairs and soon there was all kinds of shots. I didn't think he was the type to do such a thing."

"Show me."

Suddenly, the old woman's face dropped. "What? Why?"

"Because I asked you to," Kyle snapped. "Now take me up there and show me where the shots came from."

"I can tell you just as eas—"

Kyle cut her off by grabbing her arm and pulling her toward the stairs. "Do like I asked before I lose my patience with you." With that, he shoved her ahead of him so hard that she nearly tripped over the bottom step.

The old lady quickly recovered her balance and began walking up the stairs. She stumbled once or twice because she could feel Kyle right behind her like some kind of specter dogging her every move.

Although Kyle doubted he would have any trouble finding bullet holes in the hallway, he wanted to keep his eye on the old woman in case she decided to run for help or do any other such foolishness. They climbed to the top floor, which still had the leftover smell of burnt gunpowder hanging in the air.

"Right down there," she told him. "Can I go now?"

"Is Will here?"

"I don't know."

"Then go check for me."

After fussing for a few seconds, the old woman wrung her hands and shuffled down the hall to Will's door. She knocked a few times, looked back to Kyle and shrugged. "No answer," she said.

Kyle stayed right behind her, observing the pattern of the bullet holes. One thing he noticed upon closer inspection was that all of the wood was splintering outward from the door and there were no holes in the wall too far from the frame. His guess was that every one of those shots had come from the room. If any shots were sent back, they went through an open door.

"See if it's unlocked," Kyle ordered.

"I can't just—"

"I know you've got a key. Just use it and open the goddamn door."

Her hands trembling as she fumbled in the pocket of her apron, the old woman took out her master key and unlocked the door. Before Kyle said another word, she opened the door for him. The moment she turned around, she saw him bearing down on her, shoving her roughly into the room, where she tripped and fell onto the bed.

Expecting the worst, the old woman felt her breath catch in her throat and her heart tense up with a stabbing pain. The next thing she felt was the impact of something against the side of her head. After that, everything went black.

Kyle stood looking down on her with his gun still in his hand. After calmly shutting the door, he watched the woman for a few moments, until he saw that she was still breathing. A trickle of blood ran down the side of her face, but it wasn't anything too serious. He then used the corner of her apron to clean off the blood from the handle of his pistol.

Now that he had some peace and quiet, Kyle glanced around the room more carefully. He'd noticed as soon as the door opened that there wasn't anyone inside. At least, not that he could see right away. Just to be sure, he checked under the bed, which was the only real place to hide inside the room.

Nothing but dust and spiders under there.

He then began turning the room upside down, cursing under his breath once it became clear that the map wasn't there. Since Will was supposed to meet him at the Gold Coast in a few minutes, that didn't strike him as too odd. It would have been nice to get it early and in that room so there would be fewer witnesses, but killing him outside the saloon wouldn't be too much trouble.

And if Clint Adams was still around, the Gold Coast was an even better spot to meet Will. After all, it was tradition for executions to take place in public.

THIRTY-SEVEN

Clint had stormed back into Richwater with his mind sharply focused on a single goal. He was so focused that he barely even recalled leaving Eclipse at a livery before heading down the street toward the Gold Coast Saloon. His mind had cleared during the ride back into town, but his blood was still rushing through his veins.

He was no longer angry, even though he refused to let the image of those shallow graves get too far from his thoughts. Instead, he felt an urgency in his steps which didn't dissipate until he was standing in front of the saloon.

Kyle Hammund was in there.

Clint could feel it.

That was just as certain for him as the fact that the killer of those lawmen would be made to answer for what he'd done. Being able to keep himself from condemning Hammund just yet was what let Clint know he wasn't being driven by the outrage he'd felt. Even though every instinct he had said that those lawmen died for the gold at the end of that map, and no matter how much sense it made, he wasn't about to wrap that up so soon.

He had plenty of evidence to tell him what had happened and why. All he needed was that one thing that made everything undeniably clear. Clint knew he would find that last bit when he finally came face to face with Kyle Hammund. He knew that the same way that he knew Hammund was inside the Gold Coast at that very moment.

Not wanting to put it off another moment, Clint stepped into the saloon and took a look around. Being past the time when folks would eat their dinner, the place was full of a rowdier crowd and was making a whole lot more noise. Some of that noise came from the men drinking at or around the bar, while even more noise came from the girls dancing and singing on stage.

Even with all that had happened, Clint couldn't help but think back to his dinner with Josie that had taken place behind that same stage. For a moment, he wasn't sure if he was still remembering that night when he saw Josie's face again. He took a second look and found that, sure enough, she was sitting at a table near the stage, watching the show.

She wasn't expecting him, so she hadn't spotted him at the door just yet, which was what Clint preferred. With the way things might turn out, he would be even happier if she wasn't around altogether. No matter how much restraint Clint put upon himself, he doubted a killer would return the favor.

As he walked farther into the saloon, Clint looked around at the faces of all the people surrounding him. He didn't expect to pick out Hammund by recognizing his features, but he knew a murderer when he saw one. There was an unmistakable deadness in a killer's eyes that made other people feel cold when they saw it. Clint wasn't proud that he knew that fact so well, but it was a grim reality of his world.

By the time he reached the bar, Clint still hadn't spotted someone he thought could be Hammund. Rather than keep milling through the crowd and drawing attention to himself, he leaned against the bar until Sam saw he was there.

The barkeep was grinning at all the drinks he was serving and smiled even wider when he saw Clint standing nearby. "Hello there," he said as he approached and filled a mug of beer. "Didn't see you standing there. You having the usual?"

"Sure," Clint answered, even though the beer was in front of him before he made a sound. "Do you rent out the rooms here?"

"Yeah, but I think they're all full. We don't have that many and besides you might be better off at a—"

"It's not for me. I want to find Kyle Hammund. I heard he was staying here."

The name obviously struck a chord with the barkeep. Leaning in, he lowered his voice until Clint almost couldn't hear him. "You might not want to find him, Mr. Adams. Actually, it might be a good idea if you just let him be. You know what I mean? I think he's leaving tomorrow anyway."

"Where is he?"

Sam paused before answering, and took a moment to think. He might as well have just taken out an ad in the newspaper telling Clint he was about to lie to his face. "He . . . uh . . . isn't here. I actually don't know where he is."

Leaning in closer, as if to mirror Sam's own movements, Clint asked, "Then why bother lowering your voice?"

That threw Sam for a loop, and he took another second to try and come up with a suitable cover story.

"Don't even bother," Clint said, interrupting Sam's racing thoughts. "Just point him out to me and I'll take care of the rest."

"Please, Mr. Adams. I don't need anything happening to my place. I mean . . . uh . . . in my place. I don't want any trouble."

Clint didn't have any trouble picking up on the fact that the barkeep was trying his damndest to stretch out his words and speak as slowly as possible. One flick of his eyes toward the front of the room was all Clint needed from the barkeep to answer his question.

Glancing quickly over his shoulder, Clint spotted an ominous figure in a black coat heading for the door. Before leaving the saloon, however, the figure stopped and took a position next to the door, where he waited, leaning against the wall.

"Hoping to waste enough time talking for him to leave?" Clint asked with a humorless grin.

Sam tensed up at the question, but tensed even more when he saw that the man in black was still inside the saloon. "I was gonna tell you, Mr. Adams. I swear. It's just that I don't want any trouble. Especially with the sheriff not around."

Nodding, Clint took another sip of his beer, put enough money on the bar to cover the cost of the drink and said, "It's all right, Sam. I believe you. And that actually might have been a good idea. If I was you, I would want to be as far away from this as possible."

Once Clint walked away from the bar, Sam began collecting all the empty glasses and other breakables he could get his hands on.

THIRTY-EIGHT

As soon as Clint separated himself from the crowd, he saw the man in black fix his eyes on him and square his shoulders to face him. Although neither man made any sudden moves, the tension between them grew the closer Clint got. To everyone else that was drinking or talking inside the saloon, they appeared to be just one person approaching another. But that assumption would have flown out the window if they'd taken the time to look into either man's eyes.

That was where the tension could be felt so strongly that it could almost be seen, like waves of heat passing from one man to the other. A few did pick up on it and they stepped back reflexively to give both of them however much room they needed.

Clint saw those few locals move away and knew it wouldn't be long before they spread the word to their friends. Just so long as it took some of the bystanders out of the way, that was just fine with him.

When he saw Clint come to a stop in front of him, Kyle was smiling. "I'll give you credit, Adams. I didn't see you sneak in here."

"I didn't sneak anywhere, Kyle. You were probably just

too distracted waiting to get your hands on the other half of that map."

"You know all about that, huh? I guess I could be persuaded to cut you in on some of the profits if it'll make things go any easier."

Shaking his head, Clint said, "Too late for that. You chose the hard road the moment you killed those men outside of town."

"You know about the sheriff? I'm impressed."

"Actually, I didn't say it was the sheriff, and I wasn't completely sure it was you until just now."

Kyle let out a short laugh and nodded slowly. "All right, so now I'm not sneaking around anymore either. I've got my cards on the table, Adams. What now? You gonna call or fold?"

Before Clint could answer, he caught something moving in the corner of his eye. He took a quick look once he saw that Kyle was already glancing in that direction as well. Still keeping Hammund in his field of vision, Clint recognized Josie from a split-second look in her direction. It was too late to warn her to move away, since she was quickly approaching with a beaming smile on her face.

"I didn't think I'd see you so soon," she said to Clint. "What are—"

She was cut off by an iron grip around her wrist that clamped on her like a bear trap. In the next instant, she was being tugged toward Hammund, who'd taken hold of her so quickly that even Clint had barely seen it coming.

Although Clint's own hand had dropped to his Colt instinctually, he kept the pistol holstered, since he didn't want to endanger Josie any more. His eyes darted back to Hammund and locked on him with a burning intensity.

"Actually," Kyle said, "how about if I raise the stakes?" When he asked that question, his eye flicked toward Josie and his hand twitched toward his gold-plated revolver. He kept hold of her wrist just long enough to make Clint and Josie uncomfortable before he let go. Instead of drawing his pistol, he reached into a breast pocket and removed a folded piece of paper.

"Here you go, darling," Kyle said, unfolding the paper to reveal a section of a map. "Care to hold on to this for safekeeping?" Turning to Clint, he said, "That way we can talk on level ground. Sound good?"

"Keep the map," Clint said. "There's nothing you can do to make me trust you and I don't want you to drag her into this. Just let her walk away before things get any worse."

Josie was obviously scared, and she looked nervously back and forth between Clint and Kyle.

Taking a moment to let this sink in, Kyle shrugged and said, "All right." With that, his hand twitched and snapped into motion that was even faster than his previous display. The first twitch was his fist closing around the map section, and the other motion was him taking hold of Josie's arm once again and pulling her in close to his body. Not only did he get her in between himself and Clint, but he also held her out far enough to block any kind of shot from the hip that might threaten him.

All that Clint could see was a sliver of Kyle's grinning face. He might be able to hit him with a perfectly aimed shot, but to keep Josie from getting hurt, he knew he'd have to kill Hammund instantly. That might be possible if he was a little farther away, but not from the close quarters of his current position.

"I've heard a lot of things about you, Adams," Kyle said. "It seems like you're a spitfire with that pistol and a sucker for the ladies. So how about you toss that pistol or this here lady will get a broken heart."

Just then, Clint heard the muted click of a hammer being cocked behind Josie's back.

"And by that I mean, her heart'll be broken in two

when I blow it through her chest onto your shirt."

Clint could feel the rumble of feet shuffling against the floorboards all around him as everyone in sight of him and Hammund responded to Kyle's threat. That nervousness rippled through the crowd, causing everyone to back away and focus their attention onto what was going on near the front door.

Raising his voice to be heard throughout the now-quiet saloon, Kyle said, "Everyone else can just sit down and enjoy the show. I see one of you looking at me the wrong way and she's dead."

Josie was shaking in Kyle's grip, her eyes pleading with Clint as tears streamed down from them and over her cheeks. She wanted to say something, but couldn't get the words out.

Clint didn't have to hear what she wanted to say. He could already read in in her face. Although he wanted nothing more than to get her away from Hammund, he didn't want the gunman to know that he'd chosen a damn good bargaining chip.

Not only that, but Kyle had managed to get himself into a position where Clint wouldn't have had a shot even if his weapon was already drawn. For the moment, it seemed that the wrong man was holding all the aces.

THIRTY-NINE

"All right," Clint said calmly. "We can talk. And if this makes you feel better, then you can have it your way." With that, he started reaching slowly for his modified Colt.

"No," Kyle snapped. "She'll take it from you. Do it, darling. Take the gun from that holster and hand it to me."

Josie looked at Clint even as she felt the barrel of Kyle's pistol dig into her back. Only when she got a subtle nod from Clint did she lean forward and reach for the Colt. As she moved, she could feel Kyle moving behind her, keeping as much of himself behind his shield as possible.

No matter how much Clint wanted to draw and take a shot, he restrained himself. It wasn't a matter of being able to do it quickly enough. He was certain he could draw and fire before Kyle could blink. It was just that Hammund was in too good of a position.

Good for Kyle, that is, and bad for anyone trying to hit him before he sent Josie into an early grave.

Clint let her take the Colt from him and hand it over to Kyle. When the gun was tucked away beneath Hammund's coat, Clint asked, "Are you satisfied?"

"Yeah," Kyle said with a nod. "For the moment."

"Then let her go so we can talk this over like men."

"What's there to discuss? You said you didn't want any deal and I'm inclined to think that it's too late for me to offer one anyway."

"We can still make this work out in a mutually beneficial way, Kyle. There's no law around here. You saw to that. So let's talk things over before we part ways on bad terms. Just you and me."

The grin was back on Kyle's face as a laugh began to gurgle up from the back of his throat. It wasn't anything remotely humorous, but more of a way to let out some of the steam that had been building up inside of him. With the Colt sitting right where he could feel it, Kyle nodded and said, "You got balls, Adams. At least that much I heard about you is true, I can say that for sure. You got no gun, no law to back you up and nothing to barter with, but you still act like you can call some shots. That takes some balls."

"All I ask is that no more innocent blood gets spilled. Believe me, I can help you out for a fair share of the profits. Not even an equal share. Just a taste to pay me back for what I can do for you."

"And what can you do for me?"

"I can get the rest of the map for you and get the law off your tail as well."

"I'm already here to get the map."

Clint took a slow look around the saloon. "I don't see Will anywhere in here, do you?"

Only Kyle's eyes darted from side to side as a frown appeared on his face.

"He wasn't in his room either, was he?" Clint asked.

"No. Where is he?"

"Let her go and we'll discuss it over a drink."

There was a moment when Clint thought Hammund wasn't about to accept any part of the proposal. Kyle became still as a statue and his eyes were locked on Clint, as though he was studying something there that only he could see.

The rest of the saloon was holding its breath as well. Everyone in there was watching the confrontation, but was too afraid to make a sound or move a muscle. Even the dancers were frozen on stage, waiting to see what Kyle was about to do.

After another second or two dragged by, Hammund pushed Josie to one side to show he was pointing his gun directly at Clint. "Fine," he said. "Have it your way, Adams. We'll talk, but not for long. I've got business to do and killing you would just be a pleasant diversion, so it can wait for the time it takes to have one drink."

"Fair enough."

"And all of you stick around, too," Kyle said in a voice that echoed like thunder throughout the saloon. "No need to end the festivities on account of this."

Not only did the silence remain, but it actually grew thick as fog that had rolled in from a damn autumn night.

Rolling his eyes, Kyle walked over to the bar and made sure to keep Clint in front of him. He leaned against the bar and set one foot up on the dented rail, keeping the pistol at hip level. He shot a warning glare to Sam, which caused the bartender to wave excitedly to the piano player.

In a few seconds, the music started to flow and the dancers hustled off stage. Once they saw that Clint and Hammund were going to talk rather than throw down, most of the locals began speaking to each other again and got back to what they'd been doing.

Clint wished he was surprised at the callous attitude of the other people in the saloon, but he knew only too well that apart from the dancing girls, a fight was one of the most welcome shows in any saloon. He was comforted a bit to see that some of the locals were indeed making their way to the front door and slipping outside.

Standing at a spot close to the end of the bar, Clint left enough room for Kyle to step up beside him. Hammund didn't take the spot that was offered to him, however, but opted instead to stand around the corner of the bar, a couple spots away. The few locals who'd been drinking at the spots between Clint and Hammund were only too happy to step aside and let them have their space.

"Hey, Sam," Kyle said, waving for the barkeep to come closer. "Get me and my friend here a drink." Before Sam could get more than one glass in his hand, Kyle added, "And I know you keep a shotgun under the bar. Hand it over to me just to make sure it doesn't go off accidentally."

Sam reached beneath the bar, took out a sawed-off shotgun and handed it over. He gave Clint a passing glance and lowered his eyes before serving up the drinks and moving on.

Keeping one hand on his gold-plated revolver and the shotgun in his other, Kyle grinned warmly. "There. Now I can focus on business. Say your piece, Adams. I want to hear you beg for your life."

FORTY

Clint put both elbows on the bar and leaned forward as though he was just willing away an hour or two. "As much as it may disappoint you, I'm not exactly the begging sort."

"That's all right," Kyle replied. "Call it what you will."

"Actually, I'd say I'm more of a generous sort."

"Generous? Unless you've got something wrong with them eyes of yours, I'd say I'm the one holding all the cards here."

"Maybe. Maybe not."

Kyle's eyes narrowed, and some of the amusement drained from the smile he'd been wearing. "What's that supposed to mean?"

"Generous because I don't take kindly to anyone coming in and stirring up the kind of shit that you've been stirring up. I can understand you want to get a piece of some of the gold at the end of the map. Hell, I was even entertaining that idea myself until this business got too dirty and way too bloody."

"All business is dirty, Adams. And most of it's bloody too."

"Then I guess that's why I'm not a businessman." As

he spoke, Clint glanced from side to side and watched as a few more of the locals made their way out of the saloon. The place was still fairly full, but not nearly as crowded as when he'd arrived. "Certain messes involve only the men dumb enough to start them," he continued. "And that's what I thought was going on here at first.

"But then I took a closer look and found two reasons why I didn't want to try and deal with you, Will or even Eddie on your own terms. First of all, there were other hands stirring up the pot besides you three. And second, you all are too damn stupid to know when you're in over your head."

That wiped the smirk completely off of Kyle's face. "Oh, really?"

"Yeah," Clint said as he put one foot up on the bar rail. "Really."

"Well, I'm getting awful tired of this conversation, Adams. That means it's time for me to end it."

That was fine by Clint, since it appeared that he'd bought enough time for the people who wanted to get out of the saloon to do so. The muscles in his arms and legs tensed, coiling like springs in preparation for a sudden move. "You crossed the line killing those lawmen, Hammund. That was the dumbest thing you could have done because that's what made me decide to take you down rather than just let you and your partners burn through each other."

"That sheriff was dead already for all the good he did in this town. He wasn't good for anything but locking up drunks and slapping a few wrists."

"But he wasn't too dumb to track you down just in time to squash this big plan of yours, was he?"

"No," Kyle said. "But he wasn't smart enough to know I'd be coming after him, and that was the last mistake of his life."

"Funny you should mention last mistakes." Clint placed

his other foot on the rail as well, bending his knees so Hammund wouldn't noticed the step he'd taken. "You know what yours is?"

Kyle raised the sawed-off shotgun he was holding and thumbed back both hammers. "Go on and tell me, dead man."

"Talking too much."

With that, Clint pressed down with both palms against the top of the bar while pushing up with both legs. The rail was just high enough to give him a little extra clearance as he launched himself up and over the bar. His arms and shoulders burned since he'd pushed them both up to their limits in the second it took for him to make the jump. The extra effort paid off, however, as Kyle's first shotgun blast tore through the space where Clint had been standing.

Sam must have loaded the sawed-off with buckshot rather than anything larger, because Clint felt a few of the hot pellets rip through his shirt and upper arm. The wounds were nothing more than deep scratches, and the pain from them merely let him know he was lucky not to have been cut in half from such a close-up shot.

All of that flew through Clint's mind as he was still sailing through the air. The bar was directly beneath him and his legs were just coming down behind it. He straightened them out a bit and shoved off with both hands, hoping to speed his trip just a little more before the contents of that shotgun's second barrel came his way.

FORTY-ONE

Clint landed with both feet flat on the floor and let his momentum carry him the rest of the way. Letting his weight push him down beneath the bar, he folded his knees and back until he was in a huddled bundle. The moment he tucked his head in a little tighter against his chest, Clint heard the shotgun roar again.

This time, Clint could feel the heat from the blast and hear the lead slap against the wooden surface above and around him like a deadly hailstorm. Splinters rained down onto his shoulders as Clint began glancing around at his surroundings.

He knew what he was looking for, but empty glasses and bottles definitely was not it. Checking the area of the bar where Kyle had been standing turned up only more supplies, as well as a few misplaced hats and other odd items.

It had only been a second or two since Clint had made his move, but he already knew he'd let too much time go by. Sure enough, when he looked up, he saw Kyle straining his neck to look over the bar to find him. It didn't take long at all before Hammund's eyes locked onto Clint's huddled form.

Kyle climbed on top of the bar like a wild animal that smelled fresh blood. He was only halfway over, but that was enough to lean across and point his gold-handled .45 at his target.

Although he could tell Hammund was saying something, Clint's ears were ringing too much for him to hear what it was. Besides, he wouldn't have cared what the man was saying anyway, since Clint was too busy with his search. He had seen that pistol barrel staring at him like a single black eye, and he rolled backward to avoid the shot, which came a second later.

Clint felt as though the floor had been pitched at a steep angle beneath his body, as he tumbled in a ball, with his shoulders rolling first, to be followed by his lower half. Apart from the pounding of rushed footsteps, which rattled the floorboards all around him, and shouting voices, Clint could hear the .45 barking a little too close to him for comfort.

Hammund's bullet punched into the floor where Clint had started. After that, the shots kept coming, one after another, dogging Clint's trail like a fuse leading up to one final blast. He counted three shots, the last of which punched through the floor so close to him that Clint could feel the lead slicing through his leg before it drilled into the ground.

Reaching out instinctively, Clint took hold of the first thing he could find, which was a short stack of shot glasses waiting to be cleaned. He tossed the glasses toward Kyle the moment he was able and forced himself to end his roll with his body in a low crouch. When he came to a stop, Clint found himself in a worn spot of floor about halfway down the length of the bar. Not only that, but he saw a crate laying nearby, filled with the guns that Sam had collected from all the customers who'd been too drunk to leave the place heeled.

Clint let out a breath as he reached for the very thing

he'd been hoping to find since he'd jumped over the bar. He snatched up a few pistols and quickly checked the cylinders. Although neither of the guns was fully loaded, there were a few bullets in each.

Now that he had a few aces of his own, Clint rolled onto his back and turned to face Hammund. He gripped a pistol in each hand, took aim and began squeezing the triggers, just as Kyle was shaking off the barrage of glass that had been tossed at him.

Clint knew better than to fire not only with a gun in his off hand, but with two guns at once. That was not the way to hit much of anything, but it certainly was the way to make a whole lot of noise and keep Hammund from coming after him right away.

The hammer of the gun in Clint's right hand landed on one of its empty chambers, but the one in his left hit paydirt. It bucked against his palm and sent a round hissing through the air toward Hammund's forehead. Another metallic click came from the right gun as well as the left, but all Clint had to do was keep pulling the triggers to work his way to the live rounds.

It wasn't more than the space of a heartbeat or two, but it seemed like a lifetime in Clint's mind. Just as he was starting to doubt if he'd really seen those bullets in either gun, both pistols started to roar.

One after another, the guns spat out fire and smoke, filling the air with a barrage of lead. The onslaught was short, but very sweet. It replaced Kyle's smug expression with one of panic and surprise, sending him reeling so hastily that he toppled backward out of Clint's sight.

As amusing as it was to watch that, Clint kept himself focused on the task at hand. He tossed away the empty pistols and reached into the crate for some more. He settled for a Navy model Colt and a Smith & Wesson .44, which were each only missing a round or two in the chamber. Before standing up, Clint stuffed another pistol into his holster and laid a shotgun over the top of his right boot.

He stood straight up, with his right arm already pointing toward the spot where he'd last seen Hammund. Since he couldn't see the other man right away, Clint glanced around the saloon to make sure there weren't any bystanders in immediate danger.

For the most part, the customers were crouching under tables or heading for the door. A few of them had their own guns drawn, but didn't seem too eager to throw themselves into the fray. That was what separated a gunfighter from a gun owner. It took a certain sort of man to charge in when the lead was flying, and Clint could tell with a glance that he wouldn't have to worry about any of those locals stepping on his toes.

"If none of you feel like getting shot today," Clint shouted to the rest of the saloon just to be on the safe side, "then I suggest you all find your way outside."

He didn't watch to make sure they took his advice. Instead, Clint spotted a familiar face close by. The moment he spotted it, he twisted himself around to get a better look.

It seemed as though Hammund had been trying to sneak up on Clint, but wasn't able to get by without being seen. The moment he knew that he had been seen, Kyle straightened up and started squeezing off rounds from his .45.

Since Clint couldn't see the other man's gun, he knew that it was probably too low to hit him right away. That gamble might have been risky, but it paid off, and the first round Kyle fired at him dug into the thick wood of the bar. Rather than try and figure his odds again, Clint took quick aim and returned fire.

Now that he wasn't just trying to lay down some cover, Clint fired the right way and kept the gun in his second hand as a backup for when the first one went dry. His first shot clipped Hammund's shoulder, sending a crimson spray into the air that looked much worse than it truly was.

His next shot caught some more meat, at the base of Kyle's neck, but wasn't a killing blow either. Before Clint could take a third shot, he had to duck down and take a deep breath.

No matter what else Clint thought about the man, he had to admit Hammund kept his head when under fire. Not only did Kyle refuse to get rattled amid all the shots and commotion, but he gritted his teeth and plowed right through the pain of catching some lead himself. Even with blood dripping from his fresh wounds, Kyle pulled his trigger and sent enough shots into the air to drive Clint into hiding.

Keeping his head down, Clint counted the shots that punched into the wall nearby as Kyle leaned over and moved in closer. Still using that fancy gold pistol of his, Hammund was down to two shots left in his cylinder. The fifth and sixth rounds damn near caught Clint in the face, but hearing them go off was still music to his ears.

Now that Kyle's pistol was empty, Clint emptied the rest of his right gun's shells over the bar as cover, discarded it and tossed the gun over from his left to replace it. He then stood up, only to find himself staring straight down the barrel of his own modified Colt.

Even the best gambler sometimes slipped up.

FORTY-TWO

When a man was staring into the cold possibility of his own death, his mind sped up even more to soak in the moment. Perhaps it was a reflexive impulse to get in a few last thoughts before the end came, but Clint used that special clarity to pick up every bit of detail he could regarding his target.

The first thing he noticed was that Kyle had been hit a few times, but the wounds were nothing serious. The next thing he saw was that the Colt was the only gun left in Hammund's possession. Finally, Clint saw that the other man was aiming for a one-shot kill since the gun was pointed at his head rather than his chest or elsewhere on his body.

If Kyle's bullet found its mark, then it was the end of Clint Adams.

But a man's head was a whole lot tougher to hit than his torso. Especially when that man knew his head was going to be in the path of an incoming bullet.

Clint was still bringing up his own gun hand as he pulled his head down low and to the side. Squeezing off a shot less than a fraction of a second before Kyle took his, Clint made sure to keep his feet planted right where they were so he didn't cut off his last backup plan.

The round Clint had fired was hasty, but it struck Hammund in the upper body, twisting him back amid a fresh spray of blood. Even as his face contorted into a pained grimace, he aimed and fired again.

Kyle's shot hissed dangerously close to Clint's skull. The only thing that had kept it from drawing blood was the fact that Kyle insisted on a head shot rather than taking anything he could get. Clint knew he could count on that little aspect the moment he was sure Hammund was the one who'd killed those lawmen.

Every one of those corpses had been shot through the head. It was Hammund's signature as well as his weakness.

It took a second for Clint to readjust his aim since he was standing in an awkward position. Under any other circumstance, he would have fired a few rounds as his hand got into position, but he knew he didn't have many shots left. Also, he knew firearms well enough to have some reservations about putting too much faith in a weapon that had been stored in a dirty crate beneath a bar for Lord only knew how long.

The pistol could jam at any second, and since there was no room for optimism in a gunfight, Clint had to make every single shot count.

Kyle had been firing pretty steadily whenever he had Clint in his sights, but he held off for a second this time. He could tell Clint was wobbling on unsteady feet from the twisting maneuver he'd just done, and he took advantage of the slight pause to sight down the Colt's barrel and squeeze off one more shot.

There had been so many shots fired that Clint was barely twitching at the sound anymore. The smoke was thick in the air and settled in the back of his throat like bitter, gritty dust. He saw the muzzle flash from Kyle's shot and suddenly felt a hot, burning sensation slicing through his right hand.

Before Clint knew what he was doing, his fingers opened and let the gun slip from his grip. Blood poured over his hand in a hot wave, gushing from the place where he'd just been shot.

As the pistol clattered to the floor, Clint saw that Hammund was already staring at him down the barrel of the Colt. The familiar smile crept onto his face as he straightened his back out of the defensive crouch.

"Stand up, Adams," Kyle said. "You know what your problem is? You're too predictable! I only had to watch you for a few seconds to know what you'd do next."

Nodding, Clint straightened up as well, holding his hands out at waist level. *Come on*, he thought. *Build this moment up just like you want to. That's all I need.*

"So what now?" Clint asked, hoping that would be the nudge to push Hammund in the right direction.

Kyle winked and gave a single nod in response. "Now, I put you down, Adams. Right here where everyone'll see your bloody carcass."

And then it happened.

The very thing Clint had been expecting since the moment he saw that smug grin on Kyle's face. Hammund straightened his arm, held out the modified Colt for all to see and dramatically thumbed back the hammer just to hear the satisfying click as it snapped into place.

The movement was unnecessary, but for some reason Clint knew it was unavoidable. Kyle was a man who savored his kills and wasn't the type to just point and fire. There had to be a flourish, just as there had to be a signature to his previous murders. All Clint needed to do was wait for it.

When he saw what the flourish would be, Clint instantly reacted. His right leg snapped directly upward in a strong, sharp motion which sent the shotgun that had been laying there popping straight into his hands. The moment his fingers closed around the weapon, he slid his thumb over the hammers to cock them both.

Clint didn't wait for the dramatic click of the mechanism or the look on Kyle's face. Instead, he pointed and fired, sending Hammund straight to hell without any further fanfare.

It all happened so fast that Clint didn't even notice how close Hammund had gotten to pulling his own trigger. And he would never know, since the double shotgun blasts took Kyle off his feet as though he'd been hit by a train.

Despite the fact that it was empty, Clint held on to the shotgun as he walked around the bar. It kept the few others inside the saloon edging away from him rather than giving in to the foolish notion of joining the fight, to claim a piece of the action for themselves.

Clint looked at each of the potential shooters in turn, which was more than enough to get them to back off and take their hands away from their pistols. They might have been drunk or just looking for a scrap, but all the wind was out of their sails by the time Clint was standing over Kyle's body.

Lowering the shotgun, Clint reached down to retrieve his Colt from the dead man's grip. "And you said I was predictable," Clint mused.

FORTY-THREE

Although the Gold Coast was no stranger to the occasional fight or even the rare gun battle, nobody in town had seen anything like the events of that evening. Rather than clean up the mess and get on with their lives, the locals did what any self-respecting town would have done in the same position.

They retold the story to one another over drinks until early the next morning. After a few hours' sleep, they would start the whole process over again, and continue until even they were sick of hearing about all the nasty details.

The only thing on Clint's mind was getting some much-needed rest after a meal big enough to feed a small family. It wasn't until he walked out of that place that he realized he'd barely eaten throughout the entire, painfully long day.

"Hey, Adams," came a gruff, male voice from across the street.

Clint looked up and spotted Eddie Vale standing by himself, with both hands stuffed into his pockets. Walking over to the skinny man, Clint said, "I sure hope you're not mad at me, too, because I'm too damn tired to put up another fight right now."

Eddie smiled and shook his head. "Nah. I just wanted to give you my thanks is all."

"What for? Did you get ahold of that map?"

"No, but I can't say that's a bad thing. After the way I've been acting, even to one of my closest friends, I don't deserve anything that good. What I wanted to thank you for was what you did in there. I know I didn't have much time left before that mad-dog killer came after me just to shut me up for good."

Clint couldn't think of a good reason why that would have happened right offhand, but he accepted the other man's thanks anyway. Eddie seemed to lighten up only after Clint shook the hand he'd been offering.

"Also, I know Will would have been killed before me," Eddie continued. "That ain't going to happen either."

"No," Clint agreed, thinking that Eddie was at least on the mark about that one. "That's not going to happen. By the way, is Will in his room waiting this out? Maybe I should go tell him it's all right to show his face around town again."

"I just came from the boardinghouse where he stays and he wasn't there. I was hoping to catch him at the Gold Coast when all this broke out."

"Well, you're going to have to keep looking," Clint said. Suddenly, his eyes caught sight of something that made him feel as though there was a bit of steam in him after all. "And you might have to do your looking without me. At least, for tonight anyway."

Noticing the change in Clint's demeanor, Eddie turned to look at what had caught his attention. He had no trouble at all picking out Josie Moynahan as she walked slowly toward Clint with a warm, grateful smile on her face. Turning back to Clint, Eddie said, "No problem, Mr. Adams. Thanks again. Will you be in town much longer?"

"Yeah," Clint said as he opened his arms and let Josie rush forward to embrace him. "I'll be staying on for at least a little while."

Angelica watched Clint sweep that dance hall tramp into his arms and spin her around as though they'd known each other for years. Standing in the shadows beneath the awning over the Gold Coast's front entrance, the blonde stared so hard at the couple across the street that she was surprised they couldn't feel the heat of her gaze.

She'd watched the fight inside as well, her heart beating like a drum as Kyle had nearly driven The Gunsmith himself to his knees for all to see. Every shot sent a shiver through her body, until she couldn't help but let out a little moan from all the built-up tension. All the while, she'd been thinking about what she would do once she had Kyle alone again. The very thought of feeling those deadly hands on her body was almost enough to push her over the edge already.

Angelica could feel the shivers coming upon her once again, now that she was close enough to smell the leftover gun smoke which still hung in the air within the Gold Coast. It should have been her running into Kyle's arms at that moment, not watching as they carted away his body.

Watching that bitch Josie paw Clint Adams was almost enough to send another kind of shiver through her system. Unlike the ones earlier, this one was brought on by a sickness in her stomach at having to see someone like Josie get what she wanted.

Still, the more she concentrated on ignoring the dark-haired tramp, the more Angelica started to admire the man holding her. She would always miss Kyle, but even Angelica had to admit that Clint was impressive throughout the whole fight. The blonde quickly found herself moving her hands up and down over her arms as she thought about how The Gunsmith might make love to her.

She'd heard rumors about his prowess in that regard, but never really thought too much about whether or not those stories were true. Watching the way Josie reacted to his touch made her think that there might just be something to those rumors after all.

As her mind drifted to fantasies of the things she would do to Clint Adams if she got him alone, Angelica found her thoughts going back over the fight that had happened inside the saloon. She looked at it from a different angle this time, remembering the things that Clint had done and just how deadly his own hands had been.

Everyone else could keep their gold and money. Angelica preferred a man who knew how to use his hands, whether that be when they were holding a gun or moving over her bare skin. By the time Clint and Josie walked away hand in hand, Angelica had come to a decision.

She was going to get a closer look at the legendary Clint Adams before he left Richwater. Besides, she still had every intention of keeping her word to Kyle. Dead or alive, he deserved at least that much.

FORTY-FOUR

It was Sunday. Despite all the strenuous activity of the night before, Clint still managed to get himself up as the sun was rising and drag himself out of bed. Stirring slightly under the sheets, Josie shifted to watch him as he got around, not bothering to pull the blankets back over herself to cover her naked body.

"Why you up so early?" she asked groggily. "Are you that anxious to leave?"

Clint pulled on his pants and was slipping into his shirt as he turned to look at her laying there. Stretching with her arms up near her head, Josie was laying on her stomach. From where he was standing, Clint could see the uninterrupted line of her figure starting at the top of her tussled head, moving down along the sides of her breasts, over the smooth skin of her ribs and right down to the sensual curve of her buttocks and legs.

"Anxious to leave?" Clint repeated. "Right now, I'm struggling to keep from taking these clothes straight off and joining you."

Smiling mischievously, Josie shifted so that she was once again on her side and flicked the blankets completely off of her. Already, her nipples were hardening as she moved her fingers over her thigh. "Then what's stopping you?"

Clint took a moment to soak in the sight of her as well as fight back the impulse to give in to the invitation she was offering him. "I'm tempted, believe me. But I've got an appointment to keep." Putting on a sly grin of his own, Clint added, "At church. It is Sunday, you know."

Josie pouted slightly and pulled the blankets back over herself. "Well, that killed that idea."

"Sorry, but it's important."

"Well services don't start for a little while, so we can at least have some breakfast. I want to get as much of you as I can before you leave."

"Sounds like a great idea to me."

He waited for her to throw on some clothes, and then they both went to get some breakfast and coffee. Although he enjoyed the meal and company, Clint couldn't keep his mind off of the one last bit of business he needed to clear up before heading out.

FORTY-FIVE

"Ahh, Mr. Adams. I'm surprised to see you here so early. I was just going over my notes for today's services."

Clint walked up to Father Pryde, who was standing next to the church a little ways in front of the cemetery. "Actually, I've been up for a while, Father. I've even had breakfast."

"Well, that's splendid."

There were plenty of people already at the church, but most of them were standing in small groups around the front, where they were visiting with each other and Father Rayburn. More locals were streaming in, walking up to the little church with small children and family in tow.

"I'm sure I speak for the entire community when I offer my sincere thanks for all you've done," Pryde said, reaching out and shaking Clint's hand vigorously. "Sad to have it end up with so much violence, but at least it's over and that awful killer cannot hurt anyone else. May his soul rest in peace."

Clint watched Pryde and nodded slowly, bowing his head for just as long as was appropriate.

Before too long, Pryde crossed himself and said, "I hope you'll be sitting in with the rest of the congregation this morning. I've got a wonderful sermon planned."

"Is it about the love of money? That's something I'm sure you know plenty about."

Father Pryde seemed a bit put off by Clint's tone, but he shrugged and replied, "I had something else in mind, but that is a worthy subject."

"It is indeed, and I've got something that may help you."

"Really? What might that be?"

Clint reached into a jacket pocket and removed a small bundle wrapped in faded material. He tossed it into Pryde's hands and kept close watch on the other man's face.

Although he appeared to be uncomfortable, Pryde unwrapped the bundle and looked down at what was within the material. "A Bible," he said, running his hand over the front of the book, which was worn leather and stamped with faded letters. He chose to ignore the dried blood crusted on the lower edge of the binding. "How very thoughtful."

"Open it."

Pryde did so and saw an inscription written on the inside front cover.

"Read it," Clint said. "Out loud. And don't worry. Nobody's looking."

It was obvious that he didn't want any part of that inscription or the Bible on which it was written. But Pryde's eyes went back and forth between the good book and the Colt hanging at Clint's side. Swallowing hard, he read the printed words aloud. "God bless you as you tend to a flock of your own."

"Go on."

"To Father Benjamin Pryde."

"I found that on a body in some grass near here," Clint said. "It was a priest's body that was lying not too far from the sheriff and a few of his deputies."

Pryde didn't say a word. He merely looked at Clint with a blank expression on his suddenly pale face.

"Father Rayburn doesn't seem to like you much," Clint went on to say. "It's something that plenty of the locals here feel as well. Perhaps it's because you're the type of man who would pretend to be on another man's side when you were just waiting for him to get ahold of the other half of a map worth thousands, possibly hundreds of thousands, of dollars.

"Or perhaps it's because you pushed another man to hurt his best friend so you could get to that money even quicker. Turning friends like Eddie and Will against each other isn't a very Christian thing to do, is it? And whispering things into Will's ear while he was scared for his life is even worse.

"That wasn't moving fast enough for you, so you tried to get me to do your work for you. But how else were you going to get that map unless it was over one of their dead bodies? Was it easy to use Kyle Hammund like a weapon and still walk around here wearing those clothes and spouting the name of the Lord?"

Pryde fell silent and patted the front of the Bible, running his fingertips along the dried blood. "I was going to just kill Eddie or Will to get that half of the map. I'm sure Kyle wouldn't have cared who he worked for, just so long as he got his share. I ran into the priest on his way into town and he told me he was going to study under Father Rayburn and that he didn't know a soul in town."

"And it was just too good to pass up, wasn't it?"

"Yes, Mr. Adams. It was. But I swear I didn't have any part in killing those lawmen."

Smiling grimly, Clint nodded. "You know what's funny? I believe you about that. Someone gutless enough to come in and pretend to be a priest just so he didn't get his hands dirty wouldn't have the sand to draw down on armed men. You'd be able to shoot a real priest in the back, but not gun down a sheriff and his deputies. I'm sure the sheriff had probably just found the real Father Pryde's body when Hammund found him."

"So," the other man said. "What now?"

Clint turned so that he was facing the false priest head-on. He saw that someone was approaching, so he kept his voice low. "Now I want you to leave this town and these people. You're not getting any of that gold, because I know for a fact that Will's got both pieces of the map and is probably digging up that gold right now. I've met him and can say that he's got enough decency in him to cut Eddie in on it, too.

"You are a lying, cowardly piece of shit and I don't even care what your real name is. The only reason I don't want to drag you out of here myself right now is because these folks have been through enough already and don't need any more grief."

"So what do you want me to do?"

"That's simple," Clint said. "Start running, because I'll be coming after you real soon."

Suddenly, Pryde snapped his head back up again and smiled. "Mr. Adams, I'd like to introduce someone to you. I believe I told you about Miss Marple and the wonderful pies she brings for us to enjoy on this, the Lord's day?"

Clint smiled as well and lightened his tone since the churchgoers were wandering closer to them both. "I remember."

"Well, she's just arrived now." Sweeping his arm out to motion toward the front of the church, Pryde pointed Clint toward a short woman who was walking up to them carrying a pie tin covered with a linen napkin. She smiled at Pryde and even wider at Clint.

For a moment, Clint was stunned. When he'd heard about a woman who baked pies for church every Sunday, he somehow hadn't pictured her to be a curvaceous blonde with lips the shape of a bow and skin as smooth as porcelain.

Pryde smiled and said, "Clint Adams, meet Angelica Marple."

Angelica walked right up to Clint, reached up to place both hands on either side of his face and gave him a kiss on the lips which lingered only slightly beyond a casual peck. "That's to thank you for stepping in and helping while our sheriff's away. I've heard so many things about you. You're so brave."

"I'll just leave you two," Pryde said, walking away from the church with the Bible in his hands. "You two go on and talk for a bit while I put this good book somewhere safe."

And the man in priest's clothing kept walking past the locals without even stopping to return their waves. Clint knew the man would keep right on moving, because the lying bastard was too scared to do anything else.

"Actually, I've got to go as well," Clint said to the blonde. "There's some business I need to tend to."

"Sorry we couldn't have gotten to know each other better," Angelica said.

"Me, too." And with that, Clint tipped his hat and started walking toward the livery stable to retrieve Eclipse.

Angelica watched him go, feeling the Derringer pistol rubbing against her inner thigh where it was tucked away beneath a garter. She still felt the impulse to follow through on what Kyle would have wanted her to do. In fact, she'd come to that spot to put two shots directly into Clint's heart.

But now that she'd been close to him and gotten a good look at those big, deadly hands, she found she didn't want to shoot him quite so badly anymore. On the contrary, she wanted to feel him between her legs instead of that cold gun she was hiding there.

Watching him leave, she shifted from foot to foot, inching the Derringer up higher until the top of its handle grazed the lips of her moistening vagina. The shots fired the day before echoed through her head, and she focused on how Clint had moved and how he'd handled himself in the midst of so much danger.

The derringer was rubbing against a good spot, slowly inching back and forth. Angelica thought about the deadly weapon hidden beneath her skirts, giving her pleasure just as easily as it could give her death. At that moment, she decided to keep the derringer right where it was.

Clint Adams wasn't the type of man she wanted to shoot. He excited her the way only the most dangerous men did.

She would save him for later.

Watch for

LONG WAY DOWN

265th novel in the exciting GUNSMITH series
from Jove

Coming in January!